I0596069

Books by Bill Thesken

The Lords of Xibalba
The Oil Eater
Blocking Paris
Edge of the Pit
The Catalina Cabal
Exodus from Orion
Quick Read

A NOVEL

BILL THESKEN

PROLOGUE

Legend has it that in 1782 when Kamehameha the Great was a young man he went on a raid with a dozen of his warriors in Puna, on the eastern flank of the Big Island of Hawaii.

He was born in 1758 on the northern coast of the island, a land division designated Kohala, a semi-arid flat plateau bordered by a jumbled rocky coastline near a sacred temple, the Mo'okini heiau, the first temple built in Hawaii one thousand three hundred years earlier that was used for human sacrifice.

Looking northwest from his birthplace over the deep blue waters of 'Umiwai bay you can see the mountains of Haleakala rising ten thousand feet above the green jungled valleys of Maui, with the lower lying desert islands of Koho'olawe and Lanai farther to the south and west, their elevation too short to catch the rain laden trade wind clouds. To the southeast rising nearly fourteen thousand feet and keeping watch over the Big Island towers the sacred mountain of Mauna Kea.

On the night before his birth Haley's comet

passed directly over Hawaii, signifying a great event was about to happen. Since Haley's comet was sighted in December of 1758 all throughout the world, it's possible that the peak of Mauna Kea was covered in snow.

At the time of Kamehameha's birth, warring factions threatened his survival and he was hidden deep in Waipio valley until the danger passed.

Raised by his uncle, trained as a warrior, his great strength was proven when he moved the Naha stone by himself. The Naha stone, a ten foot long, three and a half ton rectangular obelisk was originally from the island of Kauai.

Legend said it washed down from the top of Mount Waialeale, then sat at the mouth of the Wailua river near the Hikinaakala Heiau until the high chief Makaliinuikualawalea placed it on a double hulled canoe and brought it to Hilo sometime around 1408.

When Kamehameha moved the stone, he proclaimed that he would conquer and unite the entire Hawaiian island chain.

He was twenty four years old at the time of the legendary raid on the seaside village in Puna.

Young, highly trained in hand to hand combat, fiercely painted faces, black tattoos across their bodies, each warrior in the pack carried a long pointed spear in one hand, and a stone knife in the other. Their target; a rival fishing village next to a small stream that emptied into the ocean.

On the beach next to the village a group of

commoners had gathered. This would be the raiding party's plunder. Some they would use for sacrifice, and the others for slaves.

The water was flowing gently, the sunlight sparkling on the surface, birds singing in the trees, as the war party made its way through the forest.

Kamehameha held up his left hand holding the stone knife, and they all stopped. He was the biggest, strongest, cruelest of them all, and they obeyed his command without question, all of them crouching and peering through the foliage while blending into the jungle.

Two slim native men wearing loin cloth were repairing a fishing net next to a dugout canoe, talking and laughing as they worked. They were directly in the path the war party must take to get to the villagers on the beach.

The great warrior motioned for the others to split with one section veering left, and the other veering right towards the beach.

The fishermen looked up from their work to see the war party ready to pounce, and shouted out to alert the people on the beach. Everyone started to run for the village, including the fishermen.

A man carrying a young child stumbled and fell on the beach, then gathered the child up to run again. The two fishermen held back, trying to distract the great warrior to let them escape.

However, Kamehameha had them in his sights, rage in his eyes. He raised his spear high in the air, prepared to throw it straight through the man with the child. Prepared to deliver the death blow stepping forward quickly, his foot slipped on the wet rocks, he stumbled, his great weight suddenly all on his left foot which crumbled the thin crust of a lava tube, the foot disappeared into the crevasse up to his knee.

He was stuck, unable to move. At the mercy of the two fishermen, who a moment ago were stricken with fear of their own imminent death, now surrounded him. One of the fishermen, named Kaleleiki grabbed a canoe paddle, stepped to the rear of the immobilized Kamehameha, and crashed the blade over his head, breaking it in half, knocking the warrior unconscious. At that point in time Kaleleiki could have killed Kamehameha, but spared his life and ran away.

The two fishermen escaped the fate of the village which was ravaged by the war party.

Twelve years later, when Kamehameha finally became King of all the islands, fulfilling his prophesy, and uniting them under his rule, he summoned the same two fishermen for punishment.

Shackled and resigned to their fate, they stood before the mighty King.

Yet instead, to the utter amazement of the royal court, Kamehameha blamed himself for attacking innocent, unarmed bystanders on that fateful day in Puna.

He gave the fishermen gifts of land and set them free. He declared a new law, "Let every elderly person, woman, and child lie by the roadside in safety."

He instituted the 'Law of the Splintered

Paddle' which protects non-combatants from harm in wartime. It was one of the first laws written into the constitution of the Kingdom of Hawaii.

Kamehameha, now king and dressed in a full length red feather cloak and headdress, flanked by stout warriors, stood before the cowering fishermen, and motioned for them to go in peace.

It's been pretty quiet since those ancient days. Nothing much going on around the Hawaiian Islands. No Kings, no war parties. No excitement. You get up, go to work, go home, go to sleep. Then you get up the next day and do it all over again.

Day, after day, after day...

It's gotten pretty boring around here.

E ho'omaka ka mo'olelo. Let the story begin.

1.

The rusty old truck lurched over the pothole filled road, rambling down the highway on one of the outer islands of the archipelago in the center of the Pacific Ocean.

Hitched to the back end was a trailer loaded with red, blue, and yellow plastic boats. Seven double man kayaks. The bottoms of the thick plastic hulls deeply scratched from years of being dragged over river stones, the tops and sides scuffed from awkward paddles glancing blows, the colors faded from intense tropical sunlight, but they were, for the most part, water tight. A couple of them might have small leaks here and there, pinholes really that might take on half a gallon per hour, but nothing that a little duct tape couldn't fix for the short term. They could handle the trip up the river at the least, then any excess water in the bottom of the hulls emptied out for the trip downstream and no one was the wiser.

Thomas O'Malley, just turned thirty, shaggy sand colored hair, an open friendly face with a bit of scruff on the cheeks from skipping a couple of days of shaving. It was a hassle to shave every day, and the tourists seemed to like the rugged look. He sipped on the coffee as he drove along the empty road, then out of the blue just hauled off and started singing.

"Sweet home Hana-maulu. Lord skies are so blue. Sweet home Hana-maulu. Lord I'm coming home to yooooou..."

He held onto the last word until he ran out of breath, letting the last notes blend out into the wind streaming through the open window, listening intently to them as they faded away. Then he let out a loud whoop and slapped the dashboard with the palm of his hand.

"Hot dang, I should be a country singer!"

It was a brand new day full of hope and adventure. The sky was clear and blue. He looked up through the windshield to double check the weather. Fluffy white trade wind clouds, not a single dark edged tyrannical rain cloud in sight. Winds from the northeast probably in the ten to fifteen range. Smooth sailing.

He was about to burst into song again when his cell phone sitting on the passenger seat rang. With one swift motion he punched the blue tooth button on the steering wheel and kept driving.

"Talk to me!" he shouted.

The voice on the other end was agitated, breathless, muffled, as though he was running through the wind. It was his best friend Kanui.

"Tom where are you..?"

"Oh, just driving down the road, passing the bridge by the old mill. Just finished singing a song. Thinking maybe I should change careers and be a famous country music singer. I should be at your house in a couple of minutes."

He passed by a homemade sign nailed to a mailbox, narrating his findings over the phone.

"Hey, check it out, there's a garage sale this morning..."

There was a rustling sound as though the phone was dropped, then the voice on the other end yelled; "Forget about the garage sale!" There was a sharp cracking sound, a 'twack' like a stick hitting an empty coconut, then Kanui shouted. "Oweee!"

"What the heck was that?" asked Tom.

"You better hurry," came the excited voice on the other end. "Cause I'm running out of golf balls. Whoops, too late!"

'What's he doing playing golf so early in the morning,' Tom wondered. Then as he came around the corner of the dirt road, the mystery was solved. Kanui's little sugar shack came into view, and there was Kanui himself, running in circles around a dilapidated old rust bucket car in the front yard with no tires, it's axles sitting high up on cinder blocks.

Chasing him around the car while throwing golf clubs like war hatchets was Kanui's hapa haole wife Tina. Her full name was Constantina Lilly Lang Kalanimoku. Most people just called her Tina for short, but Kanui always called her Constantina out of respect.

Now, Kanui was as stout a man as you would find anywhere on the island, five foot ten nearly two hundred pounds, arms like Popeye, he could climb a coconut tree with just his bare feet and hands, scamper to the top faster than an orangutan, do double back flips while cliff diving into the ocean, wrangle steers and cows, break horses, battle two or more men at once in a bar fight and always come out the winner, but up against a fire-ball tornado like his hot blooded wife he was sorely outmatched.

He had tattoos on his left arm and his right leg while the other two were bare. Whenever someone asked him about the symmetry having tats on just those two opposing appendages, he would just say they were for balance. He was a Karate champion, dabbled in Jujitsu and Tai Quan Do, but the only thing that could help him now from all of that training was defense, and quick moves.

In the corner of his eye as he ducked a well thrown golf club whizzing an inch by his ear, Kanui saw Tom's truck coming down the road and he quickly decided to leave the relative security of the rusted car, and ran out into the open, bare feet slapping down the road, hair whipped back in a self-generated wind tunnel, another well placed golf club whizzed by his head, twirling in the air like a ballerinas baton with a solid metal butt on the end. He waved wildly for Tom to catch up to him, shouting back towards the car.

"Don't slow down! Speed up, speed up!"

Kanui jumped onto the running board on the passenger's side, hanging onto the side mirror, crouched down in a defensive posture, survival in the forefront of his mind. Fear in his wild eyes that looked cautiously back, ready to either duck a missile, or fend it off with a karate chop.

"Step on it!" he yelled. "What took you so long!"

Tom shrugged his shoulders languidly. He'd seen this show before.

"I had to stop and get some coffee, you know I like a little java in the morning. Gets me going."

Kanui ducked as a nine iron went zinging by his head, landing in front of the truck which promptly ran it over, two thumps, front and rear wheels, then the trailer finished it off with a wretched clang as it got caught up under the axle, breaking it in three pieces before spitting it out past the back bumper. He looked back with sadness as the fragments skittered to a stop in the middle of the road.

"Dang, I really liked that nine iron."

Tom looked in the rear view mirror. Constantina was standing over the broken golf club, hands on her hips, heaving breaths, fiery eyes blazing at the back of the truck, she'd given up running and began kicking the ground and spitting.

"Just have it re-shafted," said Tom. "It'll be good as new."

Kanui slowly opened the passenger side door and squeezed into the seat. He was depressed, his voice soft. "Just re-shaft it, sheesh." He was silent for a few moments, staring out the side of the car as the world went by, then he sighed.

"That's a bad combo, I'm telling you."

"What is?"

"Hawaiian, Chinese, Filipino, and Italian, that's what is. And not just any Italian, but Sicilian Italian. And not just any Filipino, but the Kalingas. And not just any Chinese, no no *no*, it had to be the Mongolian brand."

"Mongolian?"

"Ever hear of Ghengis Khan? Attila the Hun?"

"Oh yeah."

"Chinese Mongolian."

Tom whistled. "Whoa."

"On their own, they're all bad ass enough, but you mix 'em all together, and pour 'em into a half pint wahine from the east side of the island, and you are looking for trouble mister."

Tom shook his head in sympathy.

"Wow, I never knew that she was part Mongolian. Didn't you do a background check or something on her? I mean c'mon now, Attila the Hun? She should have come with a warning label or something."

"Well, I'm not saying she's directly related to Attila, but sometimes..." His voice drifted off.

"What about the Hawaiian side?" asked Tom.

Kanui nearly smiled. "It seems like that's the only calming influence of the bunch."

"So, what'd you do this time," Tom chortled. "Leave the toilet seat up?"

"No, I did not leave the toilet seat up."

"Look at another girl?"

Kanui scowled, shook his head, and looked at Tom with an incredulous face, his eyes kapakai, at odd angles.

"Crazy. Are you kidding me? Look at another girl? I wouldn't be sitting here if that was the case. I wouldn't be sitting anywhere. Wouldn't have any ass cheek left to sit on. Probably be laying in a hospital bed, in a full body cast. Or maybe in a casket for the final viewing."

He sighed again, this time with his whole body sagging with the exhalation.

"Aw, it's the same old thing. Dang it. She doesn't want me to be a river boat captain."

He looked down at his dirty bare feet on the floorboards in disgust.

"She wants me to get a construction job."

Tom sighed in remorse, slowly shaking his head.

"Yeah, that really sucks."

The traffic slowed at the light, and sure enough there, right in front of them was a construction site in full swing nearby, building an addition to the bridge that had taken two years so far, and looked to be about half complete. Guys were carrying boards and metal rebar, cement trucks were lining up to pour their contents. More men with hard hats and shovels were getting ready to spread the new concrete. All of them with a fine coating of red dirt and sweat. Kanui shook his head and looked away. After all, that could be him. Sweating away, taking orders from some arrogant foreman. He couldn't bear the thought.

"I can't imagine it. I mean, I need to be the master of my own destiny, charting the waterways and keeping my bearing straight. Not punching a clock and digging a ditch. Not that there's anything wrong with that, it's just not for me."

"You should think about it carefully," said Tom. "There's a lot of different types of construction jobs. You could be an equipment operator, or a foreman, or whatever it is those guys over there are doing."

Tom pointed at two construction guys leaning on a wall and laughing at some joke one of them just told.

"You trying to get rid of me? Doesn't matter Tom. It's still a ditch. Someone else's ditch. If I'm gonna dig a ditch, it's gonna be my own ditch, dig?"

Tom laughed. "Hey I'm all for that. It's why we set up this business in the first place, right? The freedom to navigate our own destiny."

Kanui hung his head out the window, veins bulging out of his neck and shouted at the top of his lungs. "Freedom!"

The two men leaning on the wall frowned at Kanui thinking that he was mocking them. Then, when they saw who was yelling, smiled and gave him the shaka. They were practically cousins.

"That's right," said Tom. "Freedom."

"How's the gas?" asked Kanui.

They both looked at the gauge. The needle was below the empty line and the red light was beginning to flicker.

"It's fine," said Tom. "Just fine. Plenty of gas, the lights just starting to flicker, we've got at least five miles left in the tank. I'm not even sure that gauge works anymore, seems like we filled up the tank just last week, and I've only driven to the river and back. We'll do a couple of tours, get some cash, and fill 'er up later today."

A brand new sleek twelve seater van filled with tourists pulled up next to them. In gleaming black and gold letters; ALL STAR WATERFALL ADVENTURES spread from the tailgate to the front bumper with a giant gold star on the hood. Sitting in the front passenger seat was a gorgeous brunette, hair tied back in a ponytail exposing her tan skin down to her shoulders, long sharp fingernails painted bright yellow, while the driver looked like a UFC fighter on steroids wearing a wife beater t-shirt.

Bald shiny head with large protruding veins next to the temples, rippling muscles, tattooed shoulders the size of bowling balls, menacing face as though he was born with a scowl.

The girl seemed sweet as she greeted them with a wry sexy smile. But the sweetness dissipated with the gutter twang of her voice.

"Morning boys, how's it hanging?"

Tom and Kanui reluctantly glanced towards the van, hoping the traffic would move forward and get them out of here.

"Good morning Vira," said Tom.

Kanui glanced quickly at Vira. "Yeah, what he said."

The driver leaned over the steering wheel smiling at them, gap toothed, crazy eyed. His voice was thick and gruff.

"Hey dirt bags, check it out, full boat. This is how we do it in the big leagues."

Tom and Kanui's eyes scanned the length of the van. There must have been twenty tourists on board filling every seat.

Vira leaned farther out the window, smiling sweetly, batting her long black fake eyelashes.

"We could use an extra hand Kanui. If you're not too busy."

Kanui glanced over and waved her off.

"Nope, I'm all booked. Got lots of tours, a full boat. But thank you." He kept his eyes straight ahead. Last thing in the world he needed now was to get caught even talking to another girl. He looked in the side mirror just to make sure Constantina hadn't caught up to them on foot.

Grant leaned over again to get in his last two cents, yelling out the window.

"We got a couple of new jet skis too, they go great with our new water ski boat!"

Thankfully the traffic began to move.

"Well, it's sure been nice chatting with you *boys*," said Grant, emphasizing the last word.

Then with a gap toothed grin he shouted out the window. "See you on the water!"

He gunned the big block engine and passed them on the left in a cloud of exhaust. Tom and Kanui coughed, waving the smoke from their faces, while Tom gently eased the old truck forward, trying to conserve gas.

2.

The river is at its narrowest both at the top of the mountain where it all begins, and near the shore where the fresh water meets the sea.

In ancient times, this was a significant gathering place, with a prominent Heiau, a sacred temple on the point. Visiting royalty from other islands in the Hawaiian chain, and also from the far away islands of the South Pacific would oftentimes stop here first to pay their respects before venturing around the island.

A four lane steel trussed bridge spans the gap, most people traveling on the road are going too fast, and are too intent on both negotiating the crossing and avoiding the cars surrounding them to pay any attention to what is happening below them.

A sand beach extends three hundred yards north at the mouth of the river, while to the south lays a rocky point of land that curves out and around to the south.

The living structure of the river extends well out into the ocean a few hundred yards, and then inland all the way to the smallest of rivulets at the base of the mountains, and has two distinctive personalities that depend on both the weather and the tide.

Within the brackish water at the mouth of the river, that unique mixture of fresh water from the interior of the island, and the salt water from the ocean, you'll find algae, plankton, shrimp, crab, bait fish, snails, and assorted larvae for every living creature in the water.

In the summertime when the weather is dry and the water flow from the interior of the island is reduced, during low tides of minus half a foot that generally occur in the early morning hours, the sand bank where the salt water meets fresh is exposed along the course of the waterway well out onto the reef and rocky shoreline that runs to the south. The fresh water at this low tide is unimpeded and extends past the beach area out into the sea.

You can walk across the stream to the beach and only get the tops of your ankles wet.

However, on the high tides of two plus feet which occur during the late afternoon hours the brackish water extends far up into the river, the salt mixing with fresh hundreds of yards inland. At these times you can wade across the river mouth up to your chest. The salt water intrusion into the fresh water enables large ocean predators, ulua, moi, papio, mullet to venture up into the river in search of bait fish and other tasty treats, and it's not unusual to see fish in the twenty pound range, and larger, roaming within the calm confines of the waterway during these high tide events.

In the winter and spring months when the heavy rains deluge the interior of the island, nearly all the water from Mount Waialelale course down through the valleys and the plains then all are routed down through the Wailua river, the sand banks at the mouth disappear, replaced by raging black water.

Forests of driftwood, some the size of cars pile up under the trusses of the bridge wedging together in a crisscross impenetrable fortress that a beaver would be proud of, blocking the liquid flow, the water level rises behind it, widening the river over the banks up to the roots of the iron woods and hau bush growing along the sides, sometimes causing flooding in the streets and houses bordering the river. In these times it would be foolhardy to attempt a foot crossing at the mouth and would most surely result in disaster.

But now in the middle of July the river mouth is calm, the sand banks full.

The old truck eased down the dirt road towards the park and the boat launch. Kanui hard at work leaning over pushing the rear bumper while Tom is both pushing and steering at the same time with the driver's door open.

It's summertime, the weather even at this early morning hour is hot and dry. Both men sweating profusely as they push the heavy load.

They're lucky that the road inclines down rather than up, or else they would have to lug each of the kayaks half a mile to the river.

"Just a little bit further," winced Tom.

Down on the river bank, under a big brand new shining white tent marked with colorful flowing banners, Grant and Vira are watching and laughing. Their cackling filtering through the still morning air.

"Plenty of gas huh?" gruffed Kanui. The veins on his neck and arms bulging with the effort.

The old truck mercifully came to a stop. Close enough. They couldn't have moved it another inch with ten men.

"Alright," said Tom, clapping his hands and rubbing them together. "We are in business."

They could hear Grant's booming laughter magnified somehow by the water.

"Ignore him," whispered Tom to himself as he got their tent out of the back of the truck, then with Kanui struggled to get it set up. The top portion of the tent was a big white bed sheet, with four holes on the corners, supported by bamboo poles that they cut themselves up in the mountains. Stronger and more authentic that a cheap store bought tent with flimsy metal legs, bamboo was so strong you could build a house with it.

In big bold black letters on a five foot by five foot square of plywood they'd printed with magic marker:

SECRET WATERFALL ECO KAYAK TOURS $50.

Then below that in small letters so they could fit it on the sign:

Experts in Native Hawaiian Flora & Fauna.

Tom spent hours on the sign. It was the best

part of their presentation besides their own strapping good looking physical presence. It was back painted pure white with hand painted plants and animals on the edges, all along the sides danced native palms, the bottom was lined with all types of colorful fish, while on the top flew two native Hawaiian birds, a Nene Goose, and an owl, the Pueo.

They stood back to appreciate their work and high fived each other. Next, they unloaded all the kayaks from the trailer, one man at the front, one at the rear, carefully lining all seven next to each other on the river bank.

Up the river, Grant's operation was in full swing. Fifteen two man kayaks were already heading up the river, while two jet skis were zig zagging around the river banks, while the water ski boat was dragging a skier.

"Hey check it out," said Kanui, eyes big as saucers. "The new jet skis."

"Awesome," said Tom with the most unimpressed voice he could manage. "Don't worry Kanui, we'll get there. Remember Rome wasn't built in a day. We'll keep our noses to the grindstone, and succeed through hard work and determination." He punched his right fist into the palm of his left hand for effect.

An hour later they were still sitting in their beach chairs next to the kayaks and not one person had booked a tour with them. Kanui was dozing off, head tilted against the back of the chair, mouth slightly open, ready to snore at any given moment.

A young tourist family got out of their rental

car and made their way towards the park and the river.

Like a hawk eyeing its prey before pouncing, Tom studied them as they walked. It was tough to tell if they were looking to take a kayak tour, or just taking a detour on their way to some other island adventure. They looked lost, the Dad had a magazine in his hand and they were all looking down at it. He elbowed Kanui.

"Hey partner, look lively we might have some customers."

Kanui snapped out of his daydream, smoothed back his hair, and they both stood at attention next to their kayaks, ready for service.

Too late they heard the sound of the ski boat roaring down their side of the river. Vira was driving while Grant was on a single ski in the middle of the river.

The boat roared past them. Grant jumped the wake, heading straight for the shoreline, then at the last possible second banked the ski into a giant slalom turn, putting all two hundred plus pounds into it, leaning straight over onto his left shoulder, carving the ski into the glass surface.

A towering wall of water rose over Tom and Kanui as they looked up at it in dread. It seemed suspended in slow motion. Then smash, they were soaked, standing there dripping wet while Grant straightened out of his turn then looked back at them laughing. The sound of his cackling trailing behind him and lingering over the two unfortunate victims.

The family stared at them, dumfounded.

They were just about to inquire about booking a kayak tour with these two unfortunates, but now were not so sure. The father had a grim look on his face, and was slowly shaking his head. He's on vacation. Last thing he needs is to get caught up with a couple of nitwits.

One of the pre-teens was tugging on his arm, while pointing over at Grant's shiny new tent with the colorful stickers, brand new kayaks, and jet skis. They turned and walked that way. Vira turned the boat deftly in a big wide circle out on the river, then gently pulled up to the shoreline next to their tent while Grant settled his large frame into the water behind the boat, out of steam.

"Oh well," said Tom. "Lost another one. C'est la vie. Such is life."

"C'est la vie my okole," said Kanui as he gritted his teeth and started to walk towards the ski boat.

"I've got half a mind to..."

Tom reached out quickly, grabbed hold of his shoulder, and held him back.

"Whoa now tiger. Be the bigger man. There's more fish in the sea. Think about it now. You can't be a free man on the river charting the waterways and keeping your bearing straight if you're sitting in a jail cell for assault."

Kanui took a deep breath and settled down.

"Thanks Tom, sometimes I forget that I'm still on probation," he said and set himself firmly back down in his beach chair and pretended to buckle himself in.

"Probation or not, you need to harness your

emotions and stay out of trouble. Even a year from now when your probation is finished you still need to stay out of trouble. I need you next to me on the river. I can't do it without you."

Kanui was in the last year of a five year probation for busting up a couple of guys in a restaurant and putting them in the hospital.

It was early evening and the Olympic Diner on the east side was nearly empty. He was minding his own business, eating an ice cream cone, smiling and content like an old dog getting its tail bone scratched. Rocky road with a dollop of chocolate fudge on top, his favorite.

But his reputation preceded him and when one of the local ruffians walked into the restaurant with a couple of tough cowboys from an outer island he kept them in the corner of his eye while continuing his work on the ice cream.

Lopaka Apala was a big tough frazzle haired hapa-Hawaiian from the north side, although most people thought he originally came from Oahu. Not only was he tough, but he was mischievous. He sat down a couple tables away from Kanui with the cowboys and they each ordered their own pitcher of beer.

Soon, their conversations got loud and rough, and it was evident that these weren't the first beers they'd had so far that day.

Kanui could hear Lopaka tell the cowboys, "See that little guy over there? He can kick the hell out of both of you at once."

They scoffed at the notion. But it made them angry at the thought, and a slow rage boiled within them as they drank. Lopaka egged them on.

Kanui was just about finished with his ice cream, crunching down into the sugar cone. He'd been keeping one eye on the trio out of caution. He could sense trouble brewing, but he wasn't bothering anyone and wanted to finish his dessert in peace. He was here first.

The cowboys had other plans. They rose out of their chairs and approached Kanui from either side. The one on the right reached out with his hand and slapped at the cone knocking it to the floor. In the split second that the cone hit the ground, Kanui lept to his feet, kicked the chair behind him and pummeled the guy on the right with an uppercut to the solar plexus, and a left cross across his chin, knocking him clean out. Then he turned his attention to the other cowboy, who was lunging and throwing a punch his way. Too clumsy and slow. Kauni ducked under the fist, used his leverage that was moving forward by grabbing the cowboys arm, and flipped him over his hip onto a table breaking it in half with the cowboy's back. Then Kanui jumped straight onto the stunned man and finished him off with a few short ones to the ribs and jaw until the other man lay still.

Gulping for breath after the short victorious fight, Kanui stood over the two unconscious cowboys and pointed his finger at Lopaka.

"You."

"Eh, I warned them," said Lopaka. "They didn't listen. Don't mess with me Kanui. You know I'll just shoot you."

The police were there within minutes and arrested Kanui for disturbing the peace, even though it was his peace being disturbed that started the whole thing.

The cowboys didn't want to press charges, but the owner of the restaurant did. A small fiery oriental woman in her seventies, she didn't take kindly to a bunch of hooligans busting up the restaurant she and her husband spent their whole lives building into a successful, safe and welcoming environment.

The bench trial without jury was short and merciless.

"How do you plead?" the judge asked Kanui, who was so confident of his innocence that he waived legal representation.

"Not guilty your honor, they started it, I was only defending myself."

The judge interviewed all the witnesses and processed all the photo evidence into the court records, making sure his assistants catalogued everything precisely. The trial took less than forty five minutes.

A broken table, two broken noses, three broken ribs, two victims with puffy faces, one with a broken bone in his back from the judo flip onto the table, the defendant with bruised knuckles, and his very own admission under oath that he did indeed strike the victims with force intended to incapacitate them sealed his fate.

The judge's hands were tied. Even though the two cowboys were obviously out to make trouble, and had been heavily drinking which added fuel to the fire, their blood alcohol content was not measured by the attending physicians in the ER, and so any opinion as to whether they were in fact drunk was inadmissible evidence. Two drunk cowboys who wrestled steers and rode bulls picked on the wrong Hawaiian dude who knocked them both unconscious in under fifteen seconds.

Unfortunately the law was the law, and whether or not he believed that the two cowboys had it coming, which they did, he had no choice but to side with the State who brought the charges. The defendant standing in front of the court was obviously as tough as nails, and yet was honest, truthful, and respectful in all his testimony. The only thing the judge had left in his power was to somehow convince this good natured bruiser the necessity of staying far away from trouble.

The koa wood gavel pounded the matching striking block once as the verdict was announced.

"Guilty as charged," said the judge simply.

Kanui's head hung in sorrow, as he waited for his destiny which came swiftly.

At the sentencing immediately after the verdict was read into the records, the judge took all the evidence and eyewitness accounts into consideration before penalizing Kanui with five years court monitored probation, monetary compensation to the victims for the hospital bills related to their injuries, and also to the restaurant owner for the broken table.

"Someone knocked your ice cream to the

ground," said the judge. "And you nearly killed them with your bare hands. You're lucky they were a couple of tough cowboys and you didn't hurt them more severely than you did, because there is simply no justification for violence. I don't want to ever see you in this courtroom again."

Kanui took all this into consideration at the river's edge while re-buckling his imaginary seat belt, and pulling it tight.

Luckily they didn't have to wait long for a tour to come knocking on their door.

A perfect sized group of six Japanese tourists came walking their way. Grant was in his kayak leading the family tour up the river and Vira was touching up her hair in a mirror, oblivious to what was going on around her.

Not wanting to take any chances that they'd pass by for the shiny tent next door, Tom walked towards them and bowed deeply.

"Ohayou gozaimasu," he proclaimed which is the formal way to say good morning in Japanese. "And ALOOOOHAAA," he belted out while beaming, smiling ear to ear.

"Aloha!" shouted Kanui, who also bowed deep in respect. "Aloha kakahiaka! Good morning."

A seemingly full blooded Hawaiian speaking the native language to them was the hook and the tourists bowed in return, shyly approaching the bedsheet tent in awe.

3.

An half hour later Tom and Kanui paddled their kayaks next to the hau bushes along the north side of the river bank.

Following close behind, the six young Japanese tourists were happily paddling along in three of the double man kayaks. They were all chattering in their native language taking pictures as they went along.

"See," said Tom beaming with pride. "What'd I tell ya? Some happy customers. You just gotta have patience."

On the other side of the river, coming back down the other way was one of Grant's tours with Grant himself bringing up the rear, flexing his muscles with every paddle.

"Hey look," said Kanui. "There's that family that passed us up to go with the competition."

The father was in the rear seat paddling one of the kayaks. In the front a young child was screaming. He was sunburned and tired.

"My arms are tired!"

"Well stop paddling then!"

"I hate you!"

In the other kayak, the mother was struggling to paddle in the front seat, while the pre-teen in the rear seat was turning a shade of green.

"I don't feel so good," he said, then leaned over the side.

Grant was pulling up the rear of the convoy, too close to avoid the sudden spreading oil slick, and he looked with disgust as he had to dip his oar into the filthy water to keep making headway.

"Yep," said Tom. "You gotta have patience."

The river turned serene again when Grant's party faded out of sight around the bend of the river. The only sounds were the kayak paddles dipping into the soft water.

"I just love it out here," said Kanui. "The river, the sky, the jungle. I know it's kind of corny, but I fee somehow at one with nature. It kind of seeps into my core, my inner being. I sound like a hippy right?"

"You're saying what most people are afraid to admit. Publicly anyways." Tom gestured back towards their tour. "Look at them. They get it."

The Japanese tourists far behind them were laughing and chattering as they paddled. Seemingly in their own world. Tom's theory was simple, give the tourists plenty of space, don't crowd them, they came out here to unwind. There were places along the way where they needed guidance, shown which way to go, and it was in those spots that both he and Kanui conducted a sort of nature university class, describing in great detail the plants and animals that were visible in those areas, how they fit in with ecosystem, and the history of the ancient Hawaiians that co-existed with them.

The green shrouded jungle deepened as they maneuvered the kayaks down a side channel. It became eerily quiet. The tourists behind them were in awe, none of them saying a word. The shadows deepened as the trees rose taller and thicker around them.

Tom and Kanui jumped out, pulled their kayaks up onto the bank, then helped the tourists out of their boats and pulled the kayaks up alongside theirs. Deep jungle surrounded them. Tom silently motioned with his index finger to follow, and they started off down a well-worn trail. They hiked up and over a berm, shimmied over a big log covered in moss, then hopped over a couple of small brooks, and were now standing at the side of a different stream thirty yards wide, shallow light rapids over round rocks. From here they headed inland directly towards the mountain.

Theirs was an Eco Tour and they took great pride in the precise clarity of the presentation and the complete knowledge of every plant and animal on the way to the waterfall.

Even though with this particular tour they had a language barrier, they kept up their end of the bargain with a complete thorough and comprehensive tour. They stopped at the mountain apple tree where Kanui gave his Hawaiian dissertation, then up to the old silver oak tree, but the owl wasn't there. So they continued on to a cross stream, a side fork that meandered up the ridge and through a jumble of large rocks. It looked as though a giant had taken a single large boulder the size of a small mansion and smashed it in place.

Growing on the other side of the giant pile of rocks was one of Tom's favorite plants. He held up his forefinger to his lips for complete quiet while he listened intently to the surrounding forest, and scanned the entire area around them, making sure no one was nearby or watching them. On the other side of the pile of rocks, hidden from the prying eyes of the other tours that used the trail was a secret treasure.

He motioned for everyone to quickly follow him up and around to the other side of the rocks where inside of a narrow crevasse ferns of varying shapes and species nestled in the cool recesses, one of them however, was his most precious. They almost looked like ultra-green versions of maple leaves. Three pointed leaves nearly a foot wide forming a triangle on the end of a vine the size of a pencil. Some of the leaves had two extra basal lobes on the sides for a total of five.

"This," proclaimed Tom with a wave of his hand, "is the glorious Laua'e fern, *Microsorum spectrum*, endemic to Hawaii. Most of these plants around the islands have three lobes, but as you can see, some of these leaves have five, which are only found on this island. It's very rare, and this is the only plant that I know of that grows in this valley. It has a fragrance that was most sought after in the old days."

Kanui took over stating solemnly with his

local inflection while flexing his right tattooed arm for effect.

"Long ago in the distant past, when Hiʻiaka, the youngest goddess in Hawaii departed a hidden valley on the north shore with her lover Lohiʻau, she sang farewell to the steep cliffs that were made fragrant by lauaʻe ferns. She sang out; 'Aʻala ka pali i ka lauaʻe e."

"In ancient Hawaii," said Tom. "This fern was prized for its fragrance and was often used to add a pleasant scent to the tapa cloth that was used for bedding. It has a Maile scent, sort of an almond, vanilla, spicy mix. It's so rare now, that it's no longer used for hula competitions."

The tour was in awe. The leader asked in halting English if it would be okay to take a picture.

"Yes," said Tom. "But no flash."

It wasn't because the flash would harm the plant itself. He just didn't want anyone to notice the light, investigate and find the location of the fern.

Tom repeated its name for them.

"Lau'ae. You can each bend down to smell the leaf," he held out his hand and waved it back and forth, "but please do not touch."

Each in turn bowed somberly, then leaned down to get a whiff of the leaves while Kanui looked on like a sentinel from the Kings guard, eyes hardened, jaw firm, enforcing the kapu.

After each person had a turn, Tom, like the advance scout for an army, crept silently to the edge of the rocks to make sure that the coast was still clear, then he motioned for them all to follow him quickly back to the trail. This was part of the fun for the tour, doing something that was mysterious, and forbidden.

A hundred yards up the trail they passed another group that was heading back down, led by a young wiry man in bare feet.

"What's up cuz!" he shouted when he spotted Kanui and jogged straight up to him.

They shook hands and hugged, slapping each other on the back, then touched their foreheads together, the tips of their noses almost touching and breathed through them at the same time while looking straight at each other's eyes before separating and continuing on their separate ways with their tours.

In all their days they had never seen anything like it. The Japanese tourists were all beaming at Kanui, who shrugged his shoulders before explaining.

"My cousin Bully. In the old days, Hawaiians greeted each other by putting their noses close together and breathing, and we carry on the tradition from time to time. Especially up here in the valleys. When you breath together it means you have the same breath from the creator who gave us all breath. 'Ha' means the breath of life. And since we're on the subject, which we usually talk about up here, 'ha' means breath, and 'ole' means the absence of breath. You see the ancient Hawaiians who first saw the white man in the big sailing ships were amazed that they didn't greet each other with the shared breath and so they named them

Ha'ole. The term 'Ha'ole, or the way some pronounce it; Howlee, literally means without breath. But most people today just use the word haole to mean white people like Tom here."

He pointed at Tom who had a wry smile and was shaking his head.

"But you see," continued Kanui. "Tom can take it, for one thing because we all tease each other here in Hawaii, *and* he knows that he's not really a haole. He's not even a malihini which means newcomer. Tom was born on this island and spends more time up here than almost anyone. Sometimes I think Tom's more Hawaiian than me."

Tom pointed up the trail and started walking. It was time to get going again, to one of the most important parts of the journey.

A hundred yards up the trail he took a left turn, this time not bothering to make sure that no one was watching. They travelled up and over a small round hill and there in front of them was a flat area the size of a basketball court, and in the middle was a square rock wall, three feet high and the size of a two car garage.

Tom walked over with everyone following, then stood in front of the wall, reached down to touch it and left his hand on a moss covered rock the size of a bowling ball that was wedged perfectly into the top of the barrier. In fact every rock seemed as though it had been wedged perfectly in place.

"Someone put all these rocks here a long time ago," said Tom. "You can touch the rocks but be very gentle, you don't want to move them, just feel the vibrations. Feel the mana."

He was silent for many minutes as everyone in the group, Kanui included stood next to the wall and put their hands on the rocks.

The wind gently rustled the leaves in the trees high above them.

"This," said Tom, "is an ancient taro field. Whoever built this knew what they were doing. It's probably at least five hundred years old, maybe more. Some of these rocks weigh three, four hundred pounds, and came from the hillside and also from the stream bed below, rolled here and placed with care by strong men and women."

He pointed to the ten by twenty foot raised rectangle of rocks nearby, it looked like a stage, the rocks on top mostly flat.

"That, was someone's house. It would have had a thatched roof and walls, the beams cut from the Ohi'a Ai tree, the floors thatched and covered with tapa. Big enough for a family of ten. Very comfortable and dry. The forest, everything you see around us was not here back in the old days. It was all wide open. A type of native grass, called pili grew all along the hills, and this would have been a very sunny place, since taro loves sun, and the people living here loved to eat taro."

Kanui always got a little choked up when they came to this area and stayed silent, listening as Tom spoke.

"The Hawaiians came to this island at least a thousand years ago, maybe more. There's places like this all throughout these hills, little remnants of the past. House sites with taro patches. While down towards the ocean in the flat lands they've all been bulldozed to make way for sugar plantations, hotels and golf courses, residential neighborhoods, stores, shopping centers."

The slight inkling of a tear welled up in the corners of Kanui's eyes.

"But the good news is that the Hawaiians are still here, and they live in the residential neighborhoods, and work in the hotels and shopping centers. And some of them, like Kanui here, and his cousin who we saw a while ago, get to work up here."

That brought a tremendous smile to Kanui's face.

They all remained silent for a few minutes, taking in the energy, feeling the past, then Kanui turned and walked away from the wall, and they all followed as they headed back down to the trail to continue the journey to the sacred waterfall.

A clearing was up ahead, with a jungle shrouded cliff looming over the forest. They heard the sound of rushing water. A sound more violent than the stream. It got louder with every step they took. And then they could see the top of it through the trees ahead. A huge waterfall, mist curling up into the sky.

They ventured up and over the last rocky rise, and there it was. Two hundred feet high and fifty feet wide, cascading over a straight edged cliff into a giant pool filled with round rocks is the most beautiful waterfall anyone had ever seen. The Shangri-La of waterfalls.

Tom turned to the group following him, and with a big smile proclaimed:

"The secret waterfall. Hale nu Kahili."

The Japanese tourists looked like they were in shock. Eyes wide, mouths slightly open. In unison they chanted:

"Ahhhhhhhh." Unable to repeat exactly the Hawaiian word they still gave it a try. "Kahivi."

They gazed with wonder, then start snapping pictures. They bowed first for permission, then gave Tom and Kanui their cameras and posed for group shots. With three cameras around each of their necks, Tom and Kanui took turns getting just the right shot with each camera.

4.

Two glorious hours later they were back at the old truck by the river. The sky was turning orange over the island as the sun began to set. It was a successful day after all.

The Japanese tourists were all bowing and chattering, taking turns getting their pictures taken standing next to their new best friends Tom and Kanui. They've all turned giddy and a little silly with the effects of the waterfall and the incredible paddle through nature.

Then they all gathered together and started clapping.

Tom and Kanui were embarrassed at the spectacle, Kanui's tan face turned a shade of red, while Tom looked hopefully around to see if any other tourists were nearby watching the spectacle. This was great publicity.

The oldest of the group handed Tom a wad of cash while bowing deeply in respect.

Tom bowed as low as he could manage and kept the posture to emphasize deep respect and the hope for another tour in the near future, from either them, or some of their friends. Japanese tourists were renowned the world over for travelling in big groups, and if you won over a key player, you could have it made for future business.

As they walked off to their rental van, the tour guides stood together breathing a sigh of relief.

"Well," said Tom. "At least we got one good tour in today."

"It was fun," said Kanui.

"Alright," said Tom. "So, six times fifty is three hundred. We'll put twenty in the tank which should last us a couple more days. That leaves two eighty. Divided by two gives us a hundred forty bucks each. Not bad for paddling up the river eh? How long have we been here, ten hours? So, we're making fourteen an hour."

At that Tom was silent. Minimum wage for a construction worker was a lot more than that.

"Yes," said Kanui. "Fourteen bucks an hour for ten great hours on the river. Multiply that by two for the fun factor and you get twenty four per hour."

"I sure hope your wife looks at it that way," said Tom. Ever the pragmatist.

As they stood there holding their wads of cash, they got pre-occupied with thoughts about how they would be spending it, and did not hear the sound of the ski boat fast approaching.

Too late they looked up to see it passing by in front of them, a large foam vee in its wake. Vira was driving, her vibrant eyes and wry smile leading the way. Grant on the other side of the wake leaned into a long drawn out turn, then jumped the wake heading straight for them, cranking into a deep vicious turn right next to the river bank, sending another towering wall of water high into the air that cascaded down onto Tom and Kanui who were too tired to run so just stood there and took it, holding onto their wads of dripping cash.

5.

It was dark by the time they arrived back at Kanui's house. The crickets were singing in the woods, the trade winds gently brushing the leaves high in the treetops, mosquitos getting ready to pounce. The moon was soon to rise, and the light from its impending arrival lit the tops of the fluffy cumulous clouds riding high in the sky.

Tom slowed the truck and trailer to a crawl across the street. He turned off the engine and put it into neutral until the forward inertia dissipated to zero.

Silent and stealthy.

He turned the headlights off long ago, and well ahead of time, maybe a quarter mile up the road, and made sure not to press on the brakes so he wouldn't alert anyone to their presence.

The slight crunching of the tires rolling on the crushed coral along the side of the road were the only sounds they made.

The lights of the house were on, gentle music wafting from the open door. Both their sets of eyes squinted through the darkness at the warm glow flowing out of the windows while a mixture of fear, apprehension, and resignation of fate swept over them. It was over for Kanui, and they both knew it. His time had come.

"It looks safe," said Tom wistfully.

They both knew better. You could cut the tension in the air with a butter knife. Kanui had married one of the, if not *the* feistiest wahine in the entire archipelago.

One of her uncles who knew her best, since he watched her grow up from a baby, put his hand on poor Kanui's shoulder on his wedding day, shaking his head in pity, then told him that he would like to wish him luck, but it wouldn't do any good. Instead he told him simply; 'Well son, you made your bed, and now you have to lay in it.' At the time, Kanui had no idea what the old man was talking about, enthralled and enchanted by his new bride's beauty and nothing else.

"Here goes nothing," said Kanui. "Wish me luck."

"Yeah, good luck," said Tom.

"Same time tomorrow?"

"Sure," said Tom. "Seven AM. Sharp."

"Don't use that word."

"What?"

"You know," Kanui pointed to the house and made the sign of a machete on a chopping block with his two hands.

"Oh yeah. Okay, tell you what, how about I'll see you at seven AM, on the dot. How's that?"

"Alright, don't be late."

"Okay," said Tom as he put his hand on the ignition, getting ready to fire up the engine and get rolling before the fireworks started.

"Okay then," said Kanui, but he didn't move an inch from his seat.

"Stop stalling," said Tom. "You'll be okay."

Kanui reluctantly flashed the OK sign with his right hand, took a long deep breath, maybe the last one he would ever take in this life or the next, then slowly and silently got out of the truck, closed the door with barely an audible click, then watched remorsefully as Tom drove away.

He turned uneasily towards the house, gulped once, and tip toed towards it, across the road, around the rusty abandoned car sitting up on cinder blocks. He stopped for a moment to survey the scene, hesitant to leave the sanctuary of a solid object, a fortress of sorts, the car that he could hide behind, or in, if trouble erupted.

One thing stood out immediately. He'd almost forgotten about the events at the beginning of the day. All the golf clubs and balls that had been hurled his way in malice in the early morning hours were gone. They'd all been gathered up and stowed neatly back in the bag that was nestled gently against the corner of the house. He looked back down the road to see if the club that he adored, the pitching wedge still lay broken in the middle of the highway. It was also gone, hopefully tucked neatly in the bag. He made the sign of the cross, then slid over the lawn, two feet always touching the ground, finally arriving at, then creeping up the stairway, careful not to make a peep of a sound.

At the front door he stopped and surveyed the scene. He looked right, he looked left, looked quickly over his shoulder. Eyes wild, darting. He peered through the screen door. Italian music was playing on the stereo. He sniffed the air, and whispered.

"Spaghetti."

The aroma filled the air. Garlic and butter, mixed perfectly with basil and oregano, meatballs simmering, the slight hint of tomato sauce, boiling noodles, soft French bread rising in the oven, yeast and dough rounding out the fragrance of an authentic Italian dinner.

He smiled at the prospect, then his eyes narrowed with fear as he whispered again, this time with restraint.

"Spaghetti?"

Wild visions danced through his mind, scenes from gangster movies as mobsters were getting whacked in spaghetti joints, bullets flying as gangsters who one moment were sitting happily in front of plates of spaghetti, then the next moment noodles getting blown to smithereens, red sauce dripping down the sides of a table.

He heard a tiny sound from inside, like a butterflies' wings on cushioned air. Light footsteps on the other side of the door, pitter pattering soles on wood parquet floor, yet he was paralyzed, as though in a dream where his legs won't move, stuck in the sand. His wife came into view. He flinched, ready to flee for his life.

"Hi honey," she said sweetly, smiling from

ear to ear.

She was wearing a tight fitting silver silk Chinese dress with a long slit down the side to reveal her ultra-tan legs. Her luscious dark hair flowed down her back, soft shiny and inviting. She had long black eyelashes and full ruby red lips, pouting slightly, begging to be kissed. Like a super model from a glossy magazine. In short, she was a knock-out.

Kanui was shocked into action. Suddenly he was able to speak. Words actually came out of his mouth. "Hey, aren't you still mad at me?"

She scrunched her face in disappointment at the insinuation.

"Oh honey bunny, how could I stay mad at you. Now come inside, you must be tired from working all day."

She opened the door and ushered him in.

"Well, I am a little. I made some money, see?"

He reached deep into his pocket and pulled out the wad of cash, holding it in front of her with a hopeful look on his face, but she waved it away.

"You just hold onto that. Now go ahead and sit down. Go on, sit, sit."

"What am I a dog?"

"So funny."

She gently herded him over to the table and eased him into a chair, unfolded a napkin and laid it on his lap, then kissed him on the cheek and headed towards the kitchen.

"Now don't you move, I'll be right back with your dinner."

Kanui picked up a spoon from the table, using it as a mirror to look behind him for any sudden movement, or objects, whether dull or sharp, flying in his general direction.

6.

Tom got out of the truck and sauntered into the convenience store whistling. He waved to the cashier.

"Howdy Carl."

Carl frowned. "Don't you know it's bad luck to whistle at night?"

"That old wives tale?"

"Why take a chance?"

"Because I like to whistle when I'm happy, and right now I feel happy. Had a good tour today, made some cash, so I whistle."

"I'm just saying."

"Alright, so now I don't feel like whistling anymore, happy?"

Carl smiled. "If it wasn't night I'd give a whistle."

Tom got busy looking through the magazines by the register, not wanting to have his good vibe dragged down by Debbie Downer behind the counter.

"Let's see, a new Archie comic, cool. I'll also take a Mad Magazine, Sports Illustrated, Wall Street Journal, National Enquirer..."

Carl was watching intently, very interested in the selections.

"Big night on the town eh?"

"Yep, let me see, a couple of Hershey bars, some Pay Days, and how about a couple of Nutty Buddies."

"Wow, you really are living it up. Why not throw in some black licorice, and some Peppermint Patties while you're at it?"

Tom thought about it for a moment, then shook his head.

"Naw, the smell's a dead give-away."

Carl had a puzzled look on his face as he rang up the total.

"That's a whopping nineteen dollars and fifty nine cents."

Tom handed him a twenty, then in a magnanimous gesture waved the back of his hand at the cashier.

"Keep the change."

"Whoa, a tip," swooned Carl.

"Yep," said Tom. "Forty one cents my good man, you earned it, keep up the good work and there's more where that came from, I can promise you that. We'll see you tomorrow."

He walked out the door to the truck and drove up into the countryside to the old folks home. He pulled up to the well-lit concrete walled building with green tiled roof. The sign on the outside read 'Hale Kapuna'.

"Hale Kapuna," said Tom with respect in his voice. "House of the old folks."

He walked through the front door and greeted the receptionist, a middle aged woman wearing a light blue nurse's uniform. Her face lit up when she saw him.

"Well hey there Tom. They've been asking about you?"

"I had a late tour Mary, how are they doing?"

"Ornery as ever. Nora Jean won't take her medication and she still has a pain in her hip. Ray went for a little walk this afternoon, but we sent out a search party and found him before he got too far away."

"How's Doc?"

She sighed as the question slowed down her happy nature, then pursed her lips while shaking her head.

"Not good. Oh, he puts on a tough face, but he's getting weaker, you can tell. It's almost time."

Tom held up the paper bag.

"I brought him a couple of magazines to cheer him up."

"I found a candy wrapper in the trash last week," said nurse Mary. "You wouldn't know anything about that would you?"

Tom feigned shock.

"What? You think I might have brought a candy bar in here? Me?"

"It's not good for them Tom."

"I'm shocked, just shocked. So what's next, a strip search? Have at it if you want, I have nothing to hide."

He held his hands up and turned in a circle.

Nurse Mary laughed and jerked her thumb towards the door.

"Go on in ya big lug."

Tom entered the doorway. It was like a low security prison, a long hallway lined with doors to separate rooms on either side. At the end was a big open room with a giant wall mounted TV, chairs with tables, and couches. Half a dozen old people were watching TV, some in wheel chairs. He walked in and greeted them with a big smile.

"Tommy boy!" shouted an old man in a wheel chair.

"Hi handsome," said an old lady in another wheelchair.

"How's life on the outside?" wheezed an old man sitting at a table.

"It's okay," said Tom, not wanting to make them miss it. "We gotta get you out of here, and out there."

"I tried," the old man wheezed. "I went for a walk today, I was looking for a burger joint and a beer store, but they caught me and brought me back before I could find what I was looking for."

"You could have gotten lost, or hurt," admonished the old lady in the wheel chair.

"Yeah, or someone coulda stole you," laughed the old man in the other wheelchair.

"Well, they wouldn't have gotten much ransom. My bank account's all dried up. Like my skin."

Tom reached into the bag and pulled out two of the magazines.

"I brought you some reading material."

He handed the Sports Illustrated magazine to the man sitting at the table.

"There's a good article on foot speed and conditioning to help you in the sprints. Next time they won't catch you."

He handed the National Enquirer to the old lady in the wheel chair.

"Here you go Nana. Gotta keep you up to speed on the juicy gossip coming out of Hollywood, and the who's who list of alien abductions."

"Oh my," she gasped.

Tom looked around the room to make sure no one was watching and took the candy bars out of the bag. He handed them around, and the last is the Hershey bar that he put in the old lady's lap. He leaned over and whispered in her ear.

"Don't let them catch you with it. And if they do."

He made the sign of a zipper across his lips. She winked at him and also zipped her lips.

"I love chocolate, and they won't let me have any, not even a tiny bit. I'm ninety seven years old, survived a world war and a pandemic, and I can't even have a bite of chocolate now and then?" She leaned up and whispered in Tom's ear. "They're Nazis I tell you." She slipped the candy bar under the cover on her lap.

"Hey Tom, candy is dandy, but how about bringing me a big cold beer next time," said the old man in the wheel chair.

They all laughed.

"Well," said Tom. "I guess I'll go check on Doc."

No one said a word to that statement. All three of them looked away. The old man in the wheel chair shook his head slightly and then held it steady looking down at the floor.

Tom walked back down the hallway to an open door. He looked inside and knocked lightly.

"Hey Doc?"

A frail old man was lying on a bed propped up at a forty five degree angle. A tall slender oxygen tank was next to the bed with clear tubes that lead to his nostrils. His eyes were closed.

Tom walked further into the room and tried again.

"Doc?"

The old man's eyes fluttered, trying to open them, squinting towards the doorway and the sound of his name. A slight smile spread across the grey face. His voice was just north of a wheeze.

"Tom. You made it. Come in, come in. I was just resting my eyes. Sit and tell me about your day."

Tom pulled a chair from the wall and set it next to the bed.

"So tell me," continued Doc. "How was the river today? Splendid as always I'll bet."

"Still going. That water is unstoppable. I brought you a new magazine."

Tom handed the Mad Magazine to Doc who looked admiringly at the cover. His grey old eyes sparkled just a bit.

"Alfred E. Neumann. He never ages. Just look at him. Not a care in the world, never gets a day older, looks the same as he always has. If only that was the case for all of us."

He looked wistfully at the window, the light from the moon shining through the edges.

Then he continued.

"It's tough getting old. Can't move around, see the world. Sometimes I get to thinking I should have done more moving around when I was younger. Ah, but enough of that. You came to see me, tell me about your day."

Tom chuckled then got right into it.

"Well, it started out pretty uneventful, driving over to pick up Kanui, and there he was getting chased around by Constantina who's throwing golf clubs pretty accurately actually. She's a hot potato."

Doc smiled wistfully.

"I knew her Grandma. What a pistol."

"They're funny together. Hot and cold. I don't know whether to laugh or cry just thinking about them. Then we got to the river and set up shop, took a couple of hours to snag a tour but we got a good one, half a dozen Japanese tourists who just loved the journey up the river. Very respectful, and you could just see it in their eyes."

Tom knew what Doc really wanted to hear about, the waterfall, and he waited for him to ask.

"What about the falls? How are they running today?"

Tom leaned in conspiratorially. Now the conversation was getting good. "About fifty percent, just perfect. Enough to get the mist cloud going with the constant rainbow over the top of it, but not so bad as to scare you from going near it. We had lunch on the big flat rocks overlooking the pool, then we got to go halfway in for a dip. The water was cold, absolutely perfectly cold so when you got out you could almost see steam coming off your skin."

Doc looked over to the wall where a large framed photo of the waterfall hung.

"That might be the one thing I miss the most. I can see it in my mind and I can see it on the wall, but the sound of it. That's the thing you can't really capture. No audio recording could ever convey the magnitude. We tried. With the best microphones, stereo systems, giant speakers in auditoriums, we never came close. The physical presence of it. The life blood of the island cascading over the precipice, coming from the center of the ancient volcano, down through all the valleys to the falls, the final act before the gentle slope down to the sea."

The waterfall was Doc's favorite place in the whole world. Hale nu Kahili. He sighed, then looked away from the photo.

"You know Tom, you come to see me more than my own family. I really enjoy hearing about your adventures up the river. It brings me back in time, in a good way. Makes me feel alive."

"Gee Doc, you know you're like my Dad now, and have been ever since he passed away a few years ago."

"Yes, we were best of friends."

He wheezed, then pulled out the photo book

next to the bed, flipping through the pages till he came to the one he was looking for. He tapped on the full page eight by ten photo, then handed the book to Tom.

"Here we are in Hilo, forty years ago."

It was a picture of the two of them standing in front of the public library in Hilo, on the Big Island of Hawaii. In between them was a long rectangular rock about ten feet long and three feet wide on all sides. The rock was so perfectly shaped that it almost looked like it'd been carved out of the side of a cliff by a machine.

"The Naha Stone," said Tom.

"Yes, me and your Dad took a trip over to Hilo to see it. We had to see it in person, with our own eyes, not just hear about it through stories and legends. And we didn't go on any type of high society fancy-pants journey, like on an air-conditioned airplane with pretty stewardesses tucking us into our seats, or a motor boat with cold beer in the cooler. We paddled there, the whole way there and back on our single hulled sailing canoe. Battling the whole way through the roughest channels in the world. Sure we got to rely on the sail now and then, especially coming back down-wind, but I'll tell you what, that was one hellavu journey. Going upwind through the Kaiwi Channel between Molokai and Oahu nearly ended us. There's a good reason why the Hawaiians gave it that name. Kaiwi means 'the bone' and it nearly broke us in two. Took just about every bit of strength we had to get to Hilo. And there was no better way to do it either."

"Did you try to lift the stone?"

Doc smiled wryly while shaking his head. "No, even trying to wouldn't be right. We just put our hands on it to feel the mana, the power of it. You can see and feel the similarity of the rock, the density of it, the color. There's no doubt in my mind that it came from the cliff of Waialeale. And that's why we went there, in a way we were sent there on a quest to see for ourselves if it was true."

"So you really think it floated over the waterfall, and ended up on the beach at Wailua?"

Now it was Doc's turn to lean forward conspiratorially, the best he could manage in his condition.

"Now that's the thing. How *did* it get there? Because legend says that it was sitting right there at the mouth of the Wailua river when Makaliinuikualawalea put it on a double hulled canoe and sailed it to the Heiau in Hilo. Nothing in the legend says how it came to be there. It could have been hewn from the side of the mountain by the Menehune and floated down the river on a pontoon of koa trees. It could have been carried from the base of the mountain, overland through the jungle by an army of men on the tops of their shoulders."

Doc got silent for moment, settling back into the curve of the bed, well-worn and shaped by his lengthy stay. Tired from his diatribe, but still finding strength to continue.

"But what I think *might* have happened is

that it floated down a river of molten lava when the island was first being formed, straight out of the caldera at Waialeale, maybe from Kawaikini itself, the tallest peak on the island, then over the molten lava cliffs, carried to the area where the waterfall is, a waterfall of liquid rock bearing it, shaping it like a blacksmith in the fire, pounding the sides of it into ruler shaped edges until it continued onto the shoreline, finally laying there at the end of the island, smoking hot, cooling in the water where the land meets the sea, forged by the hand that formed us all, strong enough to weather the forces of nature until such a time that it travelled by the hand of man to the Big Island, which is still to this day being formed by molten lava from Mauna Loa." He smiled. "I like that story because it seems to complete a circle."

Tom took a last long look at his Dad standing next to the stone, then closed the book and handed it back to Doc.

"Wow, I've never heard that take on it."

"I don't think I've ever told that to anyone. Didn't think anyone would care, or understand what I was talking about. People might think I'm just a rambling old man. And they'd be right about it. You get to thinking about a lot of things if you're holed up with nowhere to go. At least your mind can still travel."

That made Tom smile.

"You see, this is why I like coming to visit you Doc. You always seem to have some vintage story to tell. Something you can pull right out of the archives. I don't want you to think I'm being flippant or anything, but you really are like a living treasure."

Doc waved that notion away and grunted.

"But you should be out with folks your own age more, go out and find a girl, settle down, get married."

Tom looked at the floor. That was a tough subject. One that he avoided talking about.

"Yeah well, I don't want to push it. It didn't work out the last time I tried it."

Doc shook his head.

"Ahh. That wahine used you like her own personal ATM machine, wrung you dry and then some. Left you dead broke with a pile of credit card debt that you're just now out from under. You're lucky you didn't marry her and then find out how she really was. She'd have half your house, or maybe the whole thing by now, and you'd be out on your ear with nothing. Living in the bushes all day and night. You have to put that behind you. Forget about it. It was a fluke. Happens to the best of them. Happened to me a few times in my life. I know it's hard to imagine, with me being the stud of the island and all..."

He wheezed with a half laugh, then took a minute to catch his breath enough to continue.

"...sometimes you just have to push it. There's no other way around it, maybe it's the way of the world and maybe that's how this whole comedy of human nature has been set up by our Creator. You can't always sit around waiting for fate to plunk the girl of your dreams into your lap."

"I don't even know what the girl of my dreams is anymore. I haven't a clue. She could walk right by me, and I wouldn't even know it. All I know for sure Doc, is that I want someone I can count on. I don't need any more rocky roads."

"Sometimes those are the best roads to be on," said Doc.

The old man wasn't going to let it go.

"I don't want to push it," said Tom again. "You know what I mean? Go beyond whatever I'm supposed to have in life. I figure it's probably best to just let it come to me, if it's going to come at all."

They were silent for a moment. The only sound was the oxygen slowly hissing through the tubes.

Doc continued.

"Look, all I'm saying is, next time you see an opportunity, just take it. I don't want you to get to be my age and regret that you didn't. Live it up Tommy. Just live it up."

Tom patted the side of the bed.

"Alright Doc, you got my word."

"You know Tom, your Dad was so fond of the Hawaiians and everything about them, he learned the language and could almost speak it fluently, he studied all the legends, knew which plants and animals were native, which were endemic and only found here, and which were introduced. He loved everything about these islands so much that I thought for sure he'd marry a full blooded Hawaiian wahine. Until he met that girl from Santa Barbara. She just showed up out of the blue one day. Barefoot with sunburned cheeks. On vacation, free spirited, whimsical, stunningly beautiful, and that was the end of him as far as women were concerned. Your mom really was amazing. After she passed away, he didn't even try to find another wife. Said that once you were married to the best, there was no sense trying again, because that's all it would be, trying. He put everything he had into raising you. To be the best, strongest, most resilient person possible.'

Toms mom passed away too soon, while he was still in middle school. He wondered looking at his Dad sometimes as he sat alone in the back yard in the late afternoon before sunset, looking at the fields planted deep with sugarcane, what he was thinking of.

"Your parents sure were proud of you, no doubt about that, for a lot of reasons. I think your Dad would have been most proud of you for graduating college with a degree in Botany. A degree in science, just like him."

Tom chuckled, and shook his head.

"Well, it sure took a long time. Five long years. I ran into a little roadblock course by the name of quantitative chemical analysis. Had to take it three times. And if I failed the third time I was out. I had to pass that dang course to get to the others down the line. I had to knuckle down and give it everything I had. And then I got an A of all things. From failing twice to acing it. After that everything was easy. I just finished paying off the last of my student loans and I've been out of school for seven years."

That made Doc smile.

"I'm sure it was worth the pain both financial and cerebral. You and your Dad could have had quite the conversations about all the different plants and animals up in the valleys. Maybe you could have taught him a thing or two. You probably could have talked your Mom into going up there too."

Doc wanted to ask Tom if that's why he went camping so often alone, up in the valleys. To be in some way with his parents in a spiritual sense, without the usual distractions of civilized life. But he let it go. It wasn't a question that needed to be answered. It wasn't his place. He sighed and closed his eyes, content in the moment.

Tom sat there until Doc fell sound asleep. Light whisping sounds filtering through his lips. Propped up at a forty five degree angle.

He took one more look at the picture with Doc and his Dad standing next to the waterfall and quietly let himself out of the room. Walking by the nurses station he put his two hands palms together next to his head in the universal signal of sleep. She nodded, smiling, then whispered.

"I'll check on him later."

Tom drove down the valley, onto the flat lands by the ocean, then turned into the dirt road that led to the little dark house at the end of the cul-de-sac.

His Dad left him the house when he passed

away. There wasn't much to it. Two bedrooms, one bath and a carport. Nearly a hundred years old with redwood siding and a metal roof on a scraggly quarter acre next to the old cane fields that were barren and dry now.

It wasn't much of a house, but it was paid for. And the location was epic. He could walk down a little path over a hill and be at a secluded palm tree lined beach. The land was worth ten times the house.

"Never get a mortgage," his Dad warned him. "No matter how tempting it might be to trade a piece of the house to get your hands on a pile of cash. That's how they trap you. It's like being on the wrong end of a fishing line. The end with the sharp hook on it."

"Don't worry Dad," he told him. "I won't mess up."

As he walked up the steps, two cats came slinking out of the shadows, circled his feet, purring and meowing for attention. A grey and black striped cat thin as a whip, and a giant fluffy white cat that looked like it would have a hard time climbing a tree.

"Hey there Tiger, Big Harry."

He opened the old coffee can on the washing machine and poured the dry food into two little bowls, scruffling their ears as they got to work.

He walked into the house, turned on the living room light, passed by a fish tank with three goldfish, sprinkled some food on the surface, then continued on to the kitchen.

No dishes in the sink. No food on the table. A carton of milk for the morning coffee in the refrigerator, leftover beans and a tortilla. He opened up the freezer to see the options and picked out a plastic box the size of a small bowl.

"Turkey pot pie with all the fixings."

He popped it in the microwave, set the timer for five minutes, then sat at the kitchen table with the single light bulb lamp, the lampshade was a colorful hand painted beach scene with palm trees and a hula girl in a ti-leaf skirt, turned on the radio and hummed along to a scratchy old Hawaiian tune as the mosquitos bounced against the screen door, trying to get in.

"Another day in the books Tom," he told himself trying not to be glum as he said it. "Another wonderful day."

A familiar tune came on the radio but he didn't have the heart to sing along. It suddenly felt as though it had been a long grueling day.

He felt utterly and completely alone at this point of the twenty four hour cycle and dreaded it, yet here it was again, the worst time of the day.

Mercifully the bell on the microwave binged so he could turn his attention to the matter at hand, and forget about any other feeling he was having.

Feeding the body was as important as feeding the soul he told himself, trying to make himself believe it.

7.

The next day the sunrise came again in glory, Tom was driving down the road, coffee cup in one hand, steering wheel in the other, singing a blissful song about a fair princess combing her hair by the shore.

He started every day with the same attitude, certain that it would be the best day of his life.

He passed around a curve in the road, and there up ahead was Kanui's house. This time he was running around the house being chased by his wife who had a pot and a pan in each hand. It looked like she was using the weights to her advantage leveraging them to increase her speed. Like a relay racer with two batons. Long black hair flying behind her.

Kanui disappeared behind the house in a mad scramble to escape, then abruptly re-appeared on the other side, saw Tom's truck in the corner of his eye, and made a bee line for the road, bare feet slapping on the pavement, motioning with his hand and yelling.

"Don't stop, don't stop!"

He jumped on the side runner of the truck, opened the door, deftly using it to deflect a pan that clanged off the edge, jumped into the moving vehicle, shut the door, bare feet, bare back and out of breath.

"Hey partner," he managed between gulps of air.

"Having a good morning?"

"Nothing special."

"She been chasing you since I dropped you off last night?"

Kanui shook his head, took one final deep breath, and now with his wind totally under control told his story.

"No, it's the weirdest thing. I go home and she's all dressed up, makes me dinner, being all lovey dovey and everything. Buttering me up is what she was doing. Not a single word about me getting a construction job. I roll out of bed this morning and first thing, BAM! The classifieds spread out on the table. Big yellow circles around the construction jobs. Me, I'm all dressed in shorts and t-shirt ready to go to work on the river. Where do you think you're going she asks. Why, I'm going to work, I'm going to the river with Tom, gonna do some tours. Oh no you aint she tells me. Oh yes, I am, I reply. And then the fun started. She tore the shirt right off my back, like an animal with claws, and I think I got clipped by the frying pan." He rubbed the back of his head where a little bump was starting to rise.

"You need help," said Tom.

"I don't know. Maybe I should just break down and go get the job she wants me to have."

"Sure, you could do that."

"You think?"

"Yeah, it'll make your life a whole lot easier, and that's the most important thing, don't you agree?"

"You're probably right…"

"And then someday when she decides your hair is the wrong color, you go ahead and change it to the color she wants."

"I see your point."

"And when she decides that the clothes you wear are not quite to her liking, you just hand over your pants so she can start wearing them, and you can start wearing her…"

"Okay, okay I get it."

"You have to take a stand my friend. At some point in your life you're gonna need to stand your ground, or you'll get steamrolled. That's how it works in this world that we live in, and it's about time you stepped up to the plate and admitted it."

Their conversation was abruptly interrupted by the sound of an obnoxious car horn blaring next to them. They both looked over at Vira, who was waving at them out of the brand new white SUV.

"Morning boys."

"Hey losers!" Grant shouted. "Eat this."

A sudden cloud of dust and exhaust enveloped them as Grant sped off, cutting in front of them, bits of gravel spinning off the back tires, peppering Tom's truck.

Kanui was still looking towards the driver's side, staring at Tom's profile.

"Stand your ground eh?"

"Steady as she goes," said Tom grimacing.

Later, as Tom and Kanui are sitting in their beach chairs next to the river, the tent and sign are up, the kayaks lined up waiting for customers. All the action though centers around Grant's operation. Tom is reading the newspaper.

"Maybe we just need some new equipment," he said.

"New equipment?" asked Kanui.

"Sure, some new kayaks, a couple of jet skis, and a ski boat. We'd probably attract more customers if we had a wider array of water toys."

"You're dreaming. Where are we gonna get the money to buy any of that stuff."

"Maybe we get a loan from the bank."

"A loan."

"Yeah."

"You get a loan, you gotta pay it back."

"Of course you pay it back, that's what the word loan means."

"I don't know Tom. Sounds like it'd make things a lot more complicated than they are right now."

"There's an old saying."

"What's that?"

"You have to spend money to make money."

"Yeah, spend money, not borrow money."

"We need to borrow the money first, then we spend it. See?"

"Not only are you a dreamer, you're a little whacky too."

Coming close and fast, they could hear the sound of a speedboat approaching, heading down river. Neither of them moved an inch or acknowledged its imminent arrival, then casually reached to the sides of their beach chairs, each of them pulling out and opening up an umbrella as the boat passed by in front of them, a cascade of water showering over them, Grant laughing as he exited the big turn. The boat arcing into the center of the river, circling back to their tent.

Unscathed and still dry, the two friends closed their umbrellas and put them on the side of their chairs.

Tom turned to Kanui. "What do you say we go to the bank after lunch? I know a guy."

"Sounds good to me."

Tom took a look around the park to see if any potential customers were lurking, then went back to reading his paper.

He tapped on an article towards the bottom half.

"Hey, check it out. Ashley Pepper is coming to the island."

Kanui tried to be nonchalant but stirred in his seat, nearly tweaking a muscle in his neck with the sudden unexpected motion.

"Oh yeah? Ashley Pepper? What for?"

"It says she's finishing up a new film, and might get in some R&R at the same time."

Kanui stared off into the sky, his eyes glazing over. His voice when he spoke, was decisive.

"Ashley Pepper. She's in my top five."

"Actresses?"

He shook his head and gruffed.

"Top five anything. Food, water, air, my

wife, and Ashley Pepper."

After he said her name, he snapped out of his trance, bolted upright, eyes wild looking around behind him, then sighed with relief to see that the coast was clear.

"Whoa, I'd better be careful. Constantina is crazy jealous about that wahine. How is it that a woman's intuition is so highly tuned that they know when you think another woman is just the slightest bit attractive? Whenever Ashley comes on the TV, she'll just switch the channel. I'll be like 'hey I was watching that show', and she'll be like 'well you aint watching it now', and switch to the cooking channel or something. She did it during the Super Bowl right at the end of a close game. They did one of those crowd shots, and showed Ashley in the stands, zap, gone. One of my biggest fears is that I'll blurt out her name while I'm sleeping."

"Like sleep walking?"

"Yeah like sleep walking, but this would be more like sleep talking. It my case it'd be more dangerous than sleep walking right off a cliff."

He picked up a small round stone and threw it in the water, watching the ripples spread out on the surface before continuing.

"Oh well, I guess it doesn't matter, we're not gonna see her around anyways. They usually keep the big stars sheltered from us plain 'ol common folk."

A middle aged tourist man approached them from the parking lot.

"Do you need to make an appointment?"

Tom hadn't noticed him and jumped up,

ready for action.

"No sir, first come first served."

"Where do you go in these things?"

"Well, we paddle about a mile up the river, then hike about half a mile to the most beautiful water fall you've ever seen."

"How much do you charge?"

"It's right there on the sign, fifty bucks per person, best deal in town."

"Alright, I'll take it."

"Just you?"

He waved to the parking lot.

"And them."

"Uh oh," said Tom quickly counting the heads coming out of the two vans. "Fifteen?"

"Yep, plus me makes sixteen."

"We've only got five two man kayaks. We can make two trips, or maybe some don't want to go up the river," he said hopefully.

The tourist shook his head.

"Sorry, everyone wants to go and we need to stick together."

He looked over towards Grant's tent with twenty kayaks lined up and ready to go.

Tom was crestfallen as he watched the man wave to the group who followed him down to Grant's tent.

"Well that does it," said Tom. "We're going to the bank."

8.

The sharp dressed clean shaven young man with the long pants and aloha shirt sat behind the desk looking over the loan application.

"Hmmm...." was the only sound he made for a while.

Kanui leaned towards Tom and whispered in his ear.

"Whenever a doctor makes that sound, it usually means trouble."

Doug, the bank manager took off his glasses, rubbed his eyes, then put his hands together, intertwining the fingers.

"So you need fifty thousand dollars for ten kayaks, two jet skis and a boat for water skiing. Equipment for your business on the river."

"That's right," said Kanui, smiling and trying to move it along with a positive attitude in the right direction, that would end with a loan approval.

Doug took a deep breath, and nodded, heading into the breach.

"Look guys, I've known you for a long time, we went to school together right? All the way from kindergarten to high school. So I'm going to level with you and I'm not trying to be pompous. Banks make money by loaning money. That's the business we're in. People deposit their money with us, we pay them a tiny bit of interest to use that money, and we turn around and loan that money to someone else and charge them a lot more interest to use it. We need loan money to pay off the investors, the people who deposit their money with us. It used to be easy, come in with a business proposal, a little bit of collateral, and we make the loan. Heck, sometimes you wouldn't even need any collateral, just your good name would be enough for big loans. But times have changed. The meltdown a few years ago hit everyone hard. A lot of delinquent loans had to be eaten. Banks are tighter with their money now. Loan qualifications are more strict. You need a lot of collateral, and a great business plan to get a loan. Banks need to make sure they're going to be paid back."

"So we're not getting the loan," said Tom matter of factly.

"You're just not making enough money with the business. It looks like after taxes, state park use fees, insurance, you barely have enough money left over to eat."

"Yeah," said Kanui. "But we eat really good and we could probably cut back on that. Plus if we had the extra equipment we could make more money. That's why we're here in the first place. We need new equipment so we can compete with the other, how do I say, gentlemen on the river. There's only so many tourists on the island at any given time, and right now they're going with the guy that has the shiny new penny."

Doug shook his head.

"I'm sorry guys, I know what you're up against. I just can't make a loan of this size right now. At least not at this point in time. I couldn't get it past my supervisor. If you just had a little more collateral, and little more cash in the bank as a cushion we could probably do the loan."

"If we had the cash," said Kanui. "We wouldn't need the loan."

"I know it sounds strange. I could probably get you a ten thousand dollar unsecured loan, just on your good credit alone."

"What about the kayaks we have," pressed Kanui. "Those would be collateral, and the jet skis and power boat we're going to buy, those would be collateral too."

"Banks don't like boats as collateral anymore. If you couldn't pay the loan, all we'd have is a bunch of old kayaks and a boat that we'd have to sell. Sorry guys. There is another route though."

Kanui sat forward in his chair. Tom knew where this was going and kept his back straight.

"What about the house you own Tom," said Doug. "There's a lot of ways you could use that as collateral. You could do a home equity line of credit, or even take out a conventional mortgage. Get a long term loan with a low interest rate. The money would almost be free. You take out the loan, and then pay it back as quickly as you can. If business is as good as you say it will be, it shouldn't take long."

Kanui looked hopefully over at Tom whose face was firm, eyelids drooping slightly. He shook his head slowly. "Can't do it guys."

"It's the only option," said Doug.

Tom took a deep breath. "Sorry, I made a promise." He looked over at Kanui, shrugged his shoulders and scrunched his lips, his mind was made up. It was time to go. "Well, we gave it a good try. Let's get back to the office."

Tom and Kanui headed out the bank's front door, both of them more depressed than when they walked in.

"Think we should try another bank?" asked Kanui hopefully.

"Waste of time," said Tom. "Doug's an upstanding guy. He's giving us the straight scoop. Sorry Kanui, I didn't want to say it in there, but I told my Dad I'd never get a mortgage on that house, no matter what. I promised him and that means more to me than anything else. We'll just have to dig in and work with what we got. What do you say buddy?"

Kanui slammed his fist into the palm of his hand.

"Alright let's do it. We don't need no stinking bank loan."

"That's the spirit, now let's get back to the river and kick some butt."

9.

Halfway across the Pacific Ocean, heading to Hawaii, Ashley Pepper looked out the right side window at the fluffy clouds far below the mid-sized private jet. She pressed her nose against the plexiglass window, angling her head so she could have a more direct view straight down below the wings. Finally satisfied that the blue Pacific ocean was still miles below them, the clouds above the water were still fluffy and set a proper distance from each other, and that they were still too far below to touch, she sighed and settled back in the plush leather chair. The little electronic notepad with its bright green letters set into the front wall of the cabin said they were travelling at an altitude of 42,000 feet / 7.5 miles, at 425 knots. They'd travelled 1,300 miles, and had 900 to go. They'd been flying for 2 hours 30 minutes, and their ETA was in 1 hour fifty minutes.

She had the entire plane to herself which didn't seem fair. She hoped that someone could have joined her at least for the flight over, they didn't have to spend the whole time with her on the photo shoot, but there were no takers. It was a late booking, a special request from the studio. One day of filming, two at the max for the movie she just finished. There was a script change, a request from the director for a flash-back scene. Something authentic they couldn't get in a soundstage in Hollywood. They needed a waterski sequence on a tropical river. They thought about shooting some close-ups of the boat and her skiing on Lake Havasu on the California Nevada border, then doing CGI Computer Generated Imaging for the jungle background, but the big cheese with the money shot it down. It would look fake, and turn their potential viewer base off, rather than on.

They just bankrolled a fifty million dollar action movie, and another hundred thousand wouldn't break the bank. It was an oversight, they'd find a way to write it off. Now was not the time to go cheap.

Oh well, she thought, maybe next time, if there were a next time, she could bring a friend with her. The movie business could be fickle, and even though she was a big star today, tomorrow she might be a has-been, a coat rack.

There were five empty seats on the Gulf Stream G-150. The cockpit door was closed, the pilot and co-pilot were instructed to give her ample space so she could read the two screenplays that her agent wanted her to consider. It wasn't really up to her anyways, the studio would pick the next movie for her. She knew that. Having her read the screenplays was just a ploy to make her think she had some control. Her contract was clear. Three movies, three years. She was twenty five years old when they shot the first one, and now at twenty seven, the clock was ticking louder than ever. By the time they finished the next one, she'd be twenty eight. Skin only stayed perky when it was packed with makeup under hot lights for so long. Lucky thing for her the first film was a smash hit, thirty million budget and close to a hundred million box-office. It was a rocket to fame and fortune, red carpets, A-list parties, the key to any city worldwide.

It was less than a five hour flight from L.A. direct to the little island paradise, She'd heard a lot about it, and did some research. They said it was like a garden island. Lush flower filled jungle canopies draped over ancient volcanic valleys, with rainbows and waterfalls around every corner. It sounded dreamy.

Her agent warned her.

"Get in, get the shots they want, and get out. We have your itinerary set in stone. Follow it to a capital T. We can't have any, and I mean zero deviation in your schedule. We need you back here with plenty of space to get ready for the Teen Choice Awards. Forget about the other awards shows, this is the one we need you all perky and prepped for. Those teens and pre-teens are your fans for the near future and beyond. I can't believe the studio is sending you all the way to Hawaii for a couple of minor shots this late in the game. Idiots. We have a private jet to get you there quick, and as soon as you're done we'll book you first class on the next commercial flight back to L.A."

Her agent Carol Ramirez was a no-nonsense

bullheaded dynamo, short stocky, with bright red hair, and sparkling blue eyes. Forty five years of gristled determination with the energy of a ten year old. It was joked around town that she sprinkled gunpowder on her cereal for breakfast, so she could fire off salvos at the studios on behalf of her clients.

One thing was certain. She took care of her people.

"I can't go with you since I have to babysit my other big star through another mid-life crisis, and make sure she doesn't do anything stupid. Thank goodness you're not a drama queen, and I can count on you to do the right thing and get back here pronto. Right?"

"Yes boss lady," Ashley joked.

Carol softened.

"Now listen sugar, I know you've never been to Hawaii, and it's high on your list of places to visit and vacation yada yada yada. I've been there enough times for the both of us, so I'll fill you in on the inside scoop. It's hot, crowded, overpriced, and filled with pushy transplants from the mainland that think they own the place. It's windy, sandy, the waves can get giant, and you'll sunburn the skin off your tush if you're not careful. You get in, take care of business and get back here. I know I can count on you. You're a professional." Trying to scare her in the beginning, then smooth talking her towards the end.

"Carol, don't worry."

"It's not you I'm worried about. I'm worried about one of those tan muscled beach boys with curly black hair and sparkly white smiles taking a liking to you, and you getting sweet talked by their pidgin language while they serenade you some late night with an ukulele underneath a coconut palm on the beach with the silvery moon setting into the west." She sighed and closed her eyes.

"Hmmm..." said Ashley. "I'm starting to get a picture here."

Her gruff nature returned.

"Yeah, well like I said I've been there enough for the both of us. And I've learned a few lessons along the way. You'll have your time. But later. Not now. Back to business. The studio's taking one of their director's and a film crew off a set on Maui and flying them over for your shots. One day, get in and get out."

"Who's the director?"

"Mitchell Collins. Fifty nine years old, he's been around the block a few times so he knows what he's doing. He got hot when he was young thirty years ago, then fizzled out and had to fight his way back into the business. You don't find too many guys knocking on sixties front door who are still hungry, but this guy definitely is. He's got something to prove so I don't have any doubt he can get this little photo shoot of theirs done. He might be a little pissed off that they're taking him off the Maui job for a day, but I can guarantee he won't show it. His days as a prima donna are long past. From what I hear he's all work, no play and a complete professional. So that's one more reason I feel safe sending you over there without me."

Carol pulled out the two page screenplay addendum and handed it to Ashley.

"It's a flashback. You're on vacation, doing a little waterskiing on the river, minding your own business, pure and innocent, when one of those beach boy's I told you to avoid catches your eye. He's on the side of the river watching you pass by. You smile, he smiles, you're distracted, you almost fall, but at the last possible moment manage to catch yourself, he has a genuine worried look on his face, you're embarrassed, blushing then spring back to your adoring pert and bouncy self. It's cheesy, but they want it. Maybe ten seconds at the most in the final cut if they use it at all."

"Sure seems like a lot to go through for ten seconds on the screen."

Carol smiled ruthlessly.

"Honey. This is Hollywood at its finest. You and me kiddo, we're in the big time now. Sometimes the heads of the studios have more money than brains, but who are we to say. They're the ones taking the big chances with that money, not us. They're like river boat gamblers. Sometimes it doesn't work out, and sometimes it pays off huge, and keeps on paying for years and years down the line. For them and for us. We're just along for the ride."

10.

Just after noon, Tom and Kanui were still sitting in their beach chairs next to the river.

The sting from the bank loan rejection had, for the most part, worn off, but the reality of the situation remained the same. They were in dire straits. They needed a tour if they were going to eat dinner tonight.

Both of them were getting anxious, especially Kanui since they haven't had a tour all day, and Constantina was waiting at home for him with an empty frying pan.

Strangely though, no one was at Grant's tent either. He had connections with all the tour desks at the big hotels, and usually had the bookings set up in advance, in addition to people just showing up unannounced, with no reservations.

Slow days happened for everyone, it was the fickle nature of the business.

Tom looked over at Kanui. He could see the little veins bulging near his temple as he scanned the parking lot for customers. The lot was nearly empty, with no cars on the access road headed their way.

"Don't worry Kanui. It's lunchtime. People

have other things on their minds. It'll pick up."

The river was eerily quiet. Water lapping against the rocks lining the edges. A fish jumped in the middle, the light splash audible from far away.

Diesel engines and air brakes disrupted the silence.

Two large panel trucks exited the highway, drove past the parking lot and pulled up on the grass field next to Grant's tent. A dozen hefty Samoans piled out, slid open the rear doors, and began unloading boxes and equipment. Each of them was wearing a blue t-shirt, while stenciled on the back in yellow the word GRIP.

Grant was talking with a guy wearing thick reading glasses and carrying a clipboard. He pointed something out to Grant on the clipboard. They both nodded in agreement, then walked over to the ski boat that was parked against the side of the river, lolling in the water.

The guy with the glasses scanned the area in front of them, pointing across the river to the jungle on the other side, and up at the mountain rising in the distance, the ancient volcanic caldera, the center of the island, worn down through the ages, covered in tropical rainforest, the sides and edges cut with waterfalls.

Tom and Kanui looked on with interest while trying to appear nonchalant.

Finally Kanui couldn't take it any longer and broke the ice.

"I wonder what's going on."

A couple of the grips start setting up floodlight panels, another pair unloaded tripods and cameras.

"You don't suppose," said Tom.

"Nah," said Kanui.

A long white stretch limo with tinted windows exited the highway, they could see it coming from far away heading towards the park and the river. Meandering down the access road, passing the parking lot, and stopping next to the panel trucks. The guy with the thick glasses jogged over and opened the rear passenger door.

Two perfectly shaped legs slid out, followed by a slender outstretched hand.

The guy with the thick glasses reached out to grasp it for support and out stepped the Goddess.

Wearing a short Hawaiian print dress, yellow, dotted with red hibiscus flowers, auburn hair flowing over slim tan shoulders, she smiled radiantly, surveying the entire scene around her, briefly looking over towards Tom and Kanui before her attention was taken away by the guy with the clipboard who was busy introducing her to Grant. Some tourists nearby squealed and rushed over to surround her.

Tom tried, but couldn't take his eyes off her. Some strange attraction commandeered his mind by the overall shape of her, every angle, from top to bottom, the texture and color of her hair and skin, a type of perfection that was rarely if ever seen in the fairer sex, maybe once in a lifetime if you were lucky. This woman warranted attention.

She was magnanimous in the kindness showered on her from all directions. Pure class in her elegant movements, unhurried, humble, a type of glow enveloped her, a natural beauty that couldn't be manufactured, only minted with pure gold mined from the mountains of heaven by the gods themselves. It was no wonder she was a big time movie star.

Tom was shaken out of his blissful trance by an annoying voice sitting right next to him that for some reason decided to speak.

"Did she just look at me?" wondered Kanui out loud. His voice like an airhorn at a ballet recital.

Brought back to the real world, Tom hardened his heart. "She wasn't looking at you pal, she was looking at me."

Kanui looked wildly around behind him to make sure no one was creeping up on him, He almost forgot about his number one rule about looking at, or talking about other women, no matter how innocent and sublime. It would be just his luck to have his wife show up unexpectedly, sneaking up behind him. Stranger things had happened. Seeing the coast was clear, he continued.

"I could sense a connection, a spiritual connection. Not everything has to be physical attraction, but I think between the two of us that's the icing on the cake. I could tell that she wants me. Unfortunately for her though, I'm a happily married man."

"So that's the great Ashley Pepper."

"Oh yeah," said Kanui. "In the flesh."

Tom shrugged. "Ahh. She's pretty good looking I guess, looks like she's in pretty good shape. But can you imagine the amount of maintenance required to keep that happy? A beautiful starlet? C'mon, that's gotta be a lot of work. I feel sorry for her boyfriend whoever he is. Poor schmuck."

"Yeah," said Kanui shaking his head in remorse. "I really feel sorry for that guy. Poor bastard."

"I wonder what angle Grant has in all of this. I'll bet they use his boat for the photo shoot."

"Hey, maybe they'll use his shiny bald head for extra lighting," joked Kanui.

"Naw, the top of that noggin sucks *in* all the light, like a black hole," said Tom. "The black hole of Calcutta."

"Some guys have all the luck," muttered Kanui.

"And the new boats."

Grant was talking to five tourists that were crowding around, they were asking him specific questions while motioning to the kayaks. Grant shook his head in the universal signal of sorry but no. He shrugged his shoulders, then reluctantly gestured towards Tom and Kanui. The tourists began walking towards them.

Tom smiled and slapped his hands on his knees as he jumped heartily to his feet.

"Windfall," he said. "We're in business."

Then as the tourists got closer he greeted them warmly, bowing at the waist and motioning with an open palm towards the faded yet still colorful boats in their little armada.

"Step right up folks, five in your party? Perfect, we have just the kayaks for you."

But Kanui was frowning. He whispered in Tom's ear.

"You think maybe I should hang back and watch the truck? I think I saw some vandals checking it out this morning."

"Oh gee, I don't know Kanui. What if your wife just happens to stop by unannounced and catches you watching the 'truck'?"

Kanui's brow furrowed as he thought about the potential outcome of that scenario. He looked back and forth a few times from Ashley to the highway, then shook his head with resignation.

"With my luck that's exactly what would happen." He clapped his hands together with the biggest smile he could manage. "Aloha nui loa folks, and welcome!"

11.

Out on the water, on the north side of the river, the little caravan made it way upstream, Tom leading the pack, while Kanui brought up the rear. Usually he was up front with Tom, but this time he lingered till the last possible moment. Every now and then he looked back in despair as they got farther and farther away from Ashley.

The man with the glasses who was the director for the film shoot, Mitchell Collins, was talking to Grant and Ashley and another young man.

"Ashley, I'd like you to meet Mario Cano. He's our local Hawaiian heart-throb. We brought him over from Maui with us. He's an extra on the film we're shooting over there and the studio thinks he's got the looks for the shots they need. He's your co-star in this flashback scene that we'll be filming. He's the strapping young man that took your heart long ago while you were on vacation in the South Pacific with your parents. Took your heart and broke it unfortunately, but that's the unhappy way of the world."

"Very pleased to meet you Miss Pepper, I

just loved your last movie," said Mario with a wide genuine smile as he shook her hand. He was nervous, and tried not to show it.

"Why thank you Mario. Nice to meet you too. I think you're absolutely perfect."

He did his best not to blush, although the blood rushed straight to his cheeks. The amazing beautiful Ashley Pepper just told him that he was perfect. He was just eighteen years old, but looked younger. He was a buff five feet two inches tall, a hundred twenty five pounds, shaggy black hair, bright white smile. Flawless tanned skin.

"Yes," said Mitchell. "I think he's perfect also. Just the right look for the scene we'll be shooting. I'll go over the shot list now, and then we'll get started. You know the old saying. Time is money, but you've come a long way Ashley and we need to make sure we get this right. We need two wide shots with Mario in the foreground, the river in the midground, while the jungle covered mountain looms high in the background. Everything will be in crisp focus. He'll be standing alone on the river bank watching as the ski boat passes by with Ashley doing her thing, zigging and zagging behind the boat. His body language shows that he's intrigued. Then we'll get a close up behind his head which is in soft focus, zoomed in on Ashley in sharp focus as she's looking directly towards him. We need a close-up straight shot of Mario's face with a slight enraptured smile, then another one with a look of distress, concern, then a final third shot with relief on his face. We need matching bookend shots of Ashley as she's skiing, spray in the background, also enraptured, surprised as she sees Mario, then embarrassed after she nearly crashes, then in control and beautiful again. Young and thriving and bursting with energy, gushing out of every pore. We need a bunch of running shots of Ashley water skiing, with only water in the foreground, the jungle on the other side of the river in the background, everything in sharp focus, she is zigging and zagging, nearly falling, and looking extremely good the entire time."

"I absolutely love waterskiing," said Ashley. "This should be fun."

But Mitchell did not smile. It was time for him to put down the hammer.

"Fun for you maybe, but my head is on the block if we don't get what they want."

His two stars got worried looks on their faces.

"Just kidding," he said and broke into a wide smile. "I have heard that my reputation as a director is all work and no fun. But how can this be work? We're outside, it's a beautiful day in Hawaii and we get to film some action shots. These are my favorite," he confided. "The main thing is that we have fun today. After all if we're not having fun doing this, we might as well be digging a ditch somewhere. Right? This should be the easiest one day shoot we've ever had."

He reached over to a tree nearby and knocked on the wood, then his head.

That loosened the actors up, and they relaxed.

"Mario, let's get you into makeup, I have Geena in the tent ready for you. Ashley and Grant, you come with me, let's go over the minute details of the waterski scenes."

As Mario walked out hearing range, Ashley pulled on Mitchell's elbow and whispered in his ear.

"Isn't my co-star a little young? Does he even have a driver's license?"

He laughed.

"Don't worry, you look great. Better than great. You're a couple of steps past absolutely fantastic."

Over the years, Mitchell had learned how important it was to soothe the stars to get the best out of them. If they were nervous, or unsure, it showed up on film.

She insisted.

"But he looks about ten years younger than me."

"Don't worry. We have special filters, we'll make you look sixteen, seventeen at the most. Now back to business."

He brought them down to the water's edge panning the backdrop with the outstretched pam of his hand.

"Okay, for this scene Ashley, you'll be water skiing down the river, zigging and zagging, having the time of your life, jumping the wake, and when you get to this marker here..." He pointed to a small red traffic cone hidden in the bushes by the side of the river. "Look over and smile at the camera, because that is when you first see Mario. And you, Grant, when you get to that marker..." He pointed to another marker farther down the river bank. "Crank a sharp turn towards the center of the river so we'll get a shot of the boat and skier in the frame at the same time."

"Sounds fun," said Ashley.

"Make sure you really crank the turn, get a lot of spray, a lot of action."

"You know," said Grant. "What if we did a couple of runs up the river to get her warmed up?"

"Well, I have been sitting on a plane all day, I'm kind of rusty."

"Great idea," said Mitchell. "One run up the river and back, but just in case, we'll have the cameras ready and rolling."

He waved to the crew down by the river, fiddling with the cameras.

"Greg! Are you ready?"

He got a thumbs up.

"Any time chief!"

12.

Kanui brought up the rear of the flotilla with his sad face leading the way. His last fleeting view of Ashley had long ago faded around the bend of the river, but the vision of her face remained.

The going was slow. Slogging actually. Their tour was having a tough time paddling, and it was apparent that this was the first time they'd ever tried it. This was shaping up to being the longest tour in history. At the rate they were going it would probably be a four hour tour and they'd never see Ashley Pepper again in this lifetime.

Off in the distance far downstream he could hear the faint hum of a boat engine, the sound carrying with the trade winds blowing in from the east, from the sea towards the island.

The tourists in the boats ahead of him were doing okay, getting the hang of paddling together in the two man canoes, the person in front set the pace and it was up to the rear to keep the beat of the stroke, but every now and then the paddles would clack together, the boat would veer from one side to the other and the helmsman in the rear would need to either paddle quicker on one side, or paddle backwards on the other to keep it going straight.

On the way back downstream they would be further challenged as the trade winds would be coming straight into their faces, pushing them off target with the slightest deviation of intent.

Kanui smiled thinking about the mechanics of paddling the kayak. It was in essence, pure Zen in nature. When you were paddling along, pulling your craft forward with the strength and will of your body and mind, nothing else mattered. Not the bills you had to pay, not the argument you had with your significant other, no past, no future, just the present.

He relaxed and meditated on the moment, getting into a fluid rhythm, the two sided paddle pulling one side then the other, one side then the other. No bills, no Constantina, no Ashley Pepper...

His brow furrowed, the smile turning into a grimace. She was right there, if only for a moment. He wasn't going to do anything, just look for a moment, and that moment was long gone never to be had again.

The trade winds began to strengthen, as did the sound of a power boat.

Kanui looked back and tilted his head so the sound of the engine would filter down into his ear canal. He knew the sound of that boat, and like a dog being petted on one side of his body while scratching an invisible flea on the other, Kanui instinctively reached for an umbrella that wasn't there.

The boat came roaring around the bend of the river behind them, and Kanui's grimace turned into a grin, for behind the frothing wake was not the giant bald headed Grant, but an earthly angel water skiing, zig zagging back and forth over the wake of the boat, heading their way.

Within a few moments the boat was right next to them, Grant scowling at them in the driver's seat, Ashley straightened out her turns and rode on the little wave from the wake, holding onto the handle with one hand and waving at the kayakers with her other.

Her gaze lingered on Tom a bit longer than the others as she passed and he barely managed a slight nod towards her but his face remained unsmiling.

Grant saw the exchange. His scowl turned into a mischievous grin, so he cranked suddenly down on the throttle while putting the boat into a sharp turn.

Ashley was suddenly and unexpectedly getting whipped, she put her other hand on the handle and crouched down as her speed increased, the boat had now gone well past the kayakers, and with the sudden one hundred eighty degree turn was now going downstream.

Grant headed straight towards the kayakers, then veered suddenly away. Ashley was forced by her speed to jump the wake and turn sharply to avoid the kayaks.

A wall of water drenched Tom in the lead boat. Ashley looked back mouthing the word 'sorry', but Tom was not watching, in fact he couldn't see a thing, his paddling ceased while the water streamed down his head, his wet hair covering his face.

"Typical," he whispered, as he wiped the water from his eyes. "Just typical."

13.

Grant was laughing as he headed back down the river, speed under the hull, the boat chattering on the water, the trade winds stiff in his face. He looked back at Ashley and gave her the thumbs up. She was doing great and looked comfortable on the single ski. They were heading along the south side of the river straight to the tent with the cameras rolling, the bank of lights were on.

The walkie talkie on the dashboard came to life, the producer's voice crackled.

"Alright, roll cameras. Here we go."

The cameras panned in unison as the boat passed by. Ashley concentrating on the task at hand, the physical act of skiing behind the fast moving boat, she looked towards the shoreline and saw a young man, then flashed a perfect smile at him as the boat cranked into a big round turn towards the center of the river. Ashley and the boat centered in the frame.

"Perfect!" shouted the producer. "Holy cow that was great." He pointed to Ashley as they passed by going back up stream, then holds his index finger as a question, could she do one more take right away.

She gave him the thumbs up, and he clicked on the walkie talkie.

"Alright let's do another take, then let Ashley rest."

Meanwhile, Tom, Kanui and the tourists had finally made it to the trail leading to the waterfall, and were hiking through the forest bordering the second stream.

Kanui, was pointing out all the different types of trees and plants. Even though Tom was equally if not more proficient in the biology of the area, the tourists always seemed to bond with Kanui since he looked so exotic with the tattoos, bulging muscles, wild hair, and authentic pidgin slang. He stopped in front of a giant tree. Light green ferns grew around the base of it.

"Now these ferns while native, are also found in other parts of the world. But these..."

He pointed to another type of fern nearby that looked finer, the leaves thinner, wispy. He walked over to them and motioned with dancing fingers for the rest to follow.

"... this is the palapalai fern."

He touched one of the leaves gently, reverently, and invited the others to do the same. Oohs and ahhs emanated from the guests as they watched Kanui carefully, anticipating additional significant information.

"This small fern, the Palapalai, is a very important plant in Hawaiian culture, because it's used for Hula."

He let the word sink in and they murmured after him.

"It is considered Kapu and sacred to the goddess of hula, Laka. It's used to beautify the Hula altar and the Hula dancer as well, and it is extremely sought after for making lei. Many songs and chants, called Oli, or Mele Oli, and Mele hula also mention palapalai for its beauty and cultural importance."

He moved back over to the giant tree and patted the trunk, inviting them again to do the same. This was a hands-on tour of the forest and Kanui prided himself on authenticity.

"The tree that we have towering over us, is an Ohia 'ai, otherwise known as a mountain apple. It's a canoe plant, which the ancient Hawaiians brought with them to Hawaii long ago on their double hulled canoes from the South Pacific. They used the bark to dye tapa cloth, and also for medicine, and the trunks as beams for their houses. It most likely originated in India and Malaysia, and the fruit which is quite delicious is sometimes called a Malay apple. It's scientific name is *Eugenia malaccensis*. The Hawaiians had a saying: O Hinaia`ele`ele ka malama, `aluka ka pala a ka `ohi`a."

He smiled and waited for someone to ask what it meant, then shrugged his shoulders and gave them the punch line;

"Which basically means the Mountain Apple is ripe all over the place in June."

Tom held up his hands, then put his index finger by his lips. Kanui tensed, also motioning for their tour to stay silent and not move.

Tom whispered.

"Pueo."

Then while facing the group he pointed towards his eyes with his index and middle fingers in the universal signal.

"Watch my eyes," he whispered. "Don't point at it when you see it."

Then he swiveled his head till his eyes were focused high up on the forest canopy that towered above them. One old tree, nearly a hundred foot tall, the trunk and brittle barren limbs silver with old age, like an elderly man standing on his last legs. And there, on one of the outstretched branches, sitting silently, it's body still but it's head swiveling on its axis, eyes wide, a little ball of brown feathers.

"Is that an owl?" whispered a woman.

"Yes," said Tom, taking over the wildlife presentation. This was their routine and it worked well for them, first they'd stop here at the Ohia ʻai while Kanui gave his dissertation, then if they were lucky, their little friend the Pueo owl would be at his normal perch and Tom would have his turn.

"That, dear friends, is an endemic species of barn owl, found only here in the Hawaiian islands. It's scientific name is *Asio flammeus sandwichensis*, it's a short eared owl, you really can't see its ears as they're covered in tufts of feathers."

"It looks so cute, like a little monk with its round face," whispered one of the girls.

"It's good luck to see a Pueo," said Tom. "Like the other endemic birds here in Hawaii, no one knows for sure how they got here, swept up in a wind storm traveling over thousands of miles of open ocean, perhaps landing once in a while on floating logs, feeding on small fish along the way. They feed on small mammals, insects, mice and rats."

"Eww," squeeled the little girl softly.

"Oh yeah," interjected Kanui. "One time I was watching this very owl, sitting right there in that same tree. He perked up, his eyes got wide and he dropped right off that branch, silently swooped down and picked a rat right off the ground and flew away into the forest with it dangling in its claws. That was awesome."

"Eww," the little girl whispered again, and looked carefully at the ground around her.

Tom frowned. Kanui being himself was scaring the customers.

"Mice," said Tom. "Probably came over with the first explorers, hiding in little cubby holes in the double hulled canoes, but they definitely made an entrance with the European explorers in their masted ships. They're a nuisance, not only for people, but also for native birds since they can climb tree and eat eggs. Our friend, the Pueo, is doing his job of protecting us, and the 'aina, the land that we live in. That's why we hold them in such respect. You know, I'll bet if you're all real quiet and move slowly, you can walk right up under that branch and get a better look. Just don't walk right under it if you know what I mean, give yourselves about twenty feet of space."

The group slowly walked towards the

towering tree.

"You know," said Tom to Kanui. "This is absolutely the best part of this occupation, seeing people completely immersed in nature. Look at them. We get to do this every day, and for a couple of hours they get to really unwind, while at the same time learning about a world they never knew existed. It's good for them, and it's good for us too."

"Well," said Kanui. "I think it's great that we almost have ourselves a trained owl. Just about every time we come through this route, there he is. Or maybe it's a she, I don't know. You think it's bad luck to have the tourists walk under it every time to make it leave the perch and fly?"

"Nah. There's no such thing as bad luck. Only good luck. Especially with a Pueo. Watch it show off its flying skills."

The Pueo owl watched the people approaching the giant tree intently for a moment, swiveled its head from side to side a few times, giant yellow eyes wide open, then dropped silently off the limb, swooping down and over the tourists in a magnificent glide, wings fully extended, the feathers at the ends fluttering like fingers, flapping to gain altitude again and disappeared into the forest.

They traveled to the Lauae fern, then up to the ancient house site with the taro patch, and onto the sacred falls.

14.

Grant was still chuckling to himself over Ashley spraying Tom up the river. The ski boat was parked by the river's edge. Ashley and the producer were sitting at a table in the middle of the tent, conversing with the camera crew. They were reviewing the footage that they've gotten so far on a laptop computer. The producer looked at his watch, then clapped his hands.

"Okay people, union mandated lunch break, that's a wrap. Everyone help yourselves to lunch in the tent. We'll meet back here in exactly a hour and half for the next shots."

"I'm not even hungry," said Ashley.

"You sure? We got a big spread laid out, best caterer on the island."

"No thank you," she said politely. "I usually eat a big breakfast and go through the day with a little snack. I'll have something right before we start the next shot just to pep me up."

"Hey, suit yourself, you're the star."

"I would like to go check out that waterfall everyone's been talking about. How can we get there?"

"Gee, I don't know Ashley. Isn't that kind of

far away Grant?"

"It's not too far. I can take you up there if you want. We can zip up there in the ski boat and be back in plenty of time. Fifteen minutes round trip in the boat, fifteen minutes of hiking and ten minutes of gawking, and we'll be back within an hour."

The producer looked at his watch frowning, then looked at Ashley's hopeful doe eyes and sighed.

"Okay, it's fine with me." He pointed firmly at Grant. "Just have her back within the hour, capeesh?"

"Not to worry," beamed Grant. "C'mon miss Ashley, let's go." He led her back to the boat, pulled it close to the shore so they could step in without wading in the water, lifted the sand anchor, storing it in the aft bin, fired up the engines and away they went.

Five minutes into their run up the river they carve around a bend and see a flotilla of kayaks heading downstream towards them.

"There's some kayaks up ahead," shouted Ashley over the wind. "Be careful!" She was still a little un-nerved from their last encounter.

"Don't worry," said Grant. "I'll give them plenty of room."

The speed boat passed by well to the starboard of the kayaks, everyone waving except for Tom and Grant.

Kanui with a big Hawaiian smile on his face sitting straight up at attention was specifically waving at Ashley, who recognized them from a few hours ago, and who was staring straight at

Tom who ignored her with his eyes centered squarely ahead.

"Hey," she whispered to herself. "There's the guy I accidently sprayed." She tried to get his attention, but it was too late and the flotilla faded quickly out of sight as they rounded another bend in the river.

Grant slowed the boat down, they took a turn to the right down the narrow waterway that led away from the main river.

The green jungle closed around them as they maneuvered down the channel. The only sound was the gentle hum of the motor just a hair above idle. Shadows deepening, trees rising around them.

"This is beautiful," whispered Ashley, hesitant to disturb the serenity of the moment with the sound of her voice.

Grant looked over at her and thought to himself, 'yes this is beautiful, I'm a lucky guy right now, and if I play my cards right...'

They parked the boat, Grant threw the anchor up onto the shore, nestled next to a gaggle of kayaks from another tour, and motioned for Ashley to jump off the front of the boat on the bank. He knew enough of the game to say little or nothing in a situation like this. Let the magnitude of the surroundings sink in to the pretty little lady and she'd come right around for some romance. Strong and silent, that was the key.

He led the way down the trail, Ashley following. The only sound around them was the stream flowing gently next to them and the slight roar of the waterfall that got steadily louder. They scrambled up the rocky hill, to the edge of the jungle, and out into the open, the view of the waterfall towering in front of them.

"This is incredible," Ashley whispered.

"Yep, this is what I do for work every day," said Grant.

"Can we get closer?"

"Sure follow me."

He led her down and over the rocks until they were standing next to the pool at the bottom of the falls. The edge of the mist caressing them, they could just about reach out and touch the rainbow dancing on the edge of the mist.

She turned her palms up and lifted them towards the sky, closing her eyes as the mist tickled her face.

"This is so beautiful..."

Grant, edging up next to her admired her beauty. "Yes, it is."

He leaned over and kissed her on the lips.

She opened her eyes abruptly and backed away. Her eyes wild with anger.

"What the heck are you doing?"

He shrugged his shoulders.

"What? It's just a little kiss. It's a tradition next to the sacred waterfall."

"Well I don't care if it's a tradition, I didn't ask for it, and it wasn't nice."

"You're right," said Grant. "It wasn't very nice, let's give it another try."

He moved towards her and grabbed her gently around the waist, pulling her close.

She slammed her fists against his chest, pushed him away, and pointed her finger at him.

"Get away from me, and stay away from me."

He held up his hands in surrender.

"Alright, alright. Your choice. But you don't know what you're missing."

"I'll take that chance."

He gestured towards his physique.

"This is grade A, number one prime deluxe. Never had one complaint till just now and we aim to please. Don't worry I won't try to kiss you again. I just thought you wanted it."

"Listen up hotshot. I'm going back down that trail right now, and I don't want you anywhere near me, understand?"

"Suit yourself, just don't get lost."

She turned and stomped off fuming.

Grant watched her walk off. He murmured to himself.

"Oooh, I'm a big star, don't touch me. Cold as ice if you ask me. Like kissing an iceberg. She'll be back, oh yeah, they always come back, and I'll thaw that berg."

He picked up a flat rock and skipped it across the pool towards the cascading water.

Off in the distance and out of sight under a line of trees, a young couple having a picnic have been watching.

"Lover's quarrel?" asked the man.

"How in the world could anyone come to a place like this and be mad at each other?" wondered the woman.

"I hope you don't ever get mad at me like

that if I give you a little kiss," he said.

"Aww, boochie woochie..." she cooed and tweaked his lips.

Meanwhile, Ashley is still fuming while stomping down the trail.

"Grade A number one argghhhhh! I just wanted a moment, just one little moment to enjoy nature without someone snapping a picture, or telling me where to line up or how to smile, or *pawing* at me!"

The fumes coming from her anger so obscured her thinking that she didn't realize where she was. She stopped at a fork in the trail. It didn't look familiar. In fact, nothing looked the same as she remembered it.

"Was there a fork in the trail?"

The little stream that she'd been hiking next to was long gone, and now there was this odd fork in the trail. One leading left, and one leading right. She looked at one, then the other. Pointed at the left with her left finger, then turned and pointed at the right with her right finger, then turned around to face the direction of the waterfall. There is no sound of water, she's traveled out of earshot. She turned in a circle, walked backwards, then looked towards the fork in the trail again, nodding her head as she made up her mind.

"Yep, it's the one on the left."

She started down the trail.

"Wait."

She turned back facing the way she'd come.

"No, it's definitely the other one."

She headed down the trail to the right,

satisfied with her decision. She slowly began to calm down as the magnificent scenery surrounded her. Birds were whistling in the tree tops. She paused to locate the source, looking with wonder at the life flitting around the canopy, birds of all shapes and sizes hopping from branch to branch.

She continued down the path, reaching out to touch the leaves as she passed. Sunlight streaming through the jungle. The trail angled slightly upwards. She came to the edge of a valley. This was a new sight.

"I took the wrong turn."

She continued just a little bit farther to look down into the valley.

"Oh my gosh," she whispered, stunned.

Right below her, shimmering in the forest light was a small waterfall cascading gently into a pool of blue water.

She looked back at the trail.

"I should probably head back."

Her eyes were drawn to the little waterfall.

"It doesn't look that far away, and I haven't been gone that long. I just want to take a little dip in that pool. I may never be back this way again in my entire life."

She made up her mind, striking off the trail, pushing against the thicket of ferns.

It wasn't long before the vegetation got thicker and higher, obscuring her vision, tall ferns pressing against her face towering five feet over her head. Strange vines with sharp hooks like cats claws grabbed and tugged at her clothes and then her arms and legs, they seemed almost alive, when just a tiny bit of their thin surface latched on to her, the more she tried to escape and extract herself from their grasp, the more they advanced as with a will of their own. She decided it was best to avoid that type of weed altogether, and plan ahead where to sidestep them.

She stopped, suddenly afraid that she may never find her way back to the trail, but as she looked back could see that there was a visible cut where she's pushed through the jungle. It should be no problem following her path back to the trail.

She listened carefully. In the distance she could hear the faint sound of the waterfall, the water gently cascading over rock into a pool.

She smiled, newly energized, pushing ahead, spreading the ferns apart with willing hands, struggling against them.

The going got tougher, the plants thicker now wedged as though in a plot against her perfect plan to move quickly through them, intertwining now like rope, or a web from a giant green spider. There appeared to be no way forward. Her quest was at a standstill.

Ashley though was hard headed to a fault, and the ferns have met their match. She took a deep breath, summoned her inner chi, solidified her core muscles, tightening them in a ball below her sternum, flexed her arms and crashed headlong against her adversary. Her strength is too much and the wall of ferns gave way. All the way. Suddenly there was only air in front of her. The path forward is finally clear, she could see that she was at the edge of a mud covered slope. No more pesky ferns to hinder progress, but her forward momentum so tremendous and strong cannot be stopped. She grasped at the last remaining fern leaves behind her to keep from falling, but it was too late. She fell forward with a thump on the slope, tumbled once, ending up on her rear end feet forward sliding down the hill.

She picked up speed, a human toboggan heading down a mud covered ski slope, digging her heels in to try to slow down, there was a bump in the slope ahead, she hit it full speed, flying through the air again, flailing her arms and landed in a deep pool of cold clear water.

She was elated, still alive.

"That wasn't so bad," she said.

Now though, she was caught in a current, the seemingly benign pool of water was in reality a small torrent, shoes slipping against the moss covered rocks. There was no way to get a foothold, she was moving quickly forward.

"I can't get out."

Up to her chin in the water, barely keeping her head above the surface she can't make headway towards the shore. The current picked up steam now carrying her along with it. She was traveling quickly down the stream, which is heading for an infinity type edge. She can see the sky right down onto the edge of the water in front of her which is rapidly approaching. In a blur her mind drifted off. Her house in Malibu has an infinity edge. It drops off the side into a pool below. This is what she is barreling towards. She flailed against the turbulent water, shoes slipping on rocks. Frantic now. Her life passing before her eyes. She went over the edge, and yet it's not a cliff that she's riding over, it's a lava tube half pipe slanting down at a forty five degree angle, covered in moss, now free from the encompassing liquid she picked up speed on the smooth jelly surface of the green moss, flying twenty feet out into the air then landing in the deep pool below.

She struggled underwater, surrounded by dark green water and bubbles, the undertow gone, but dragged down by both the momentum of her plunge and the weight of her shoes and clothes, reaching the rock strewn bottom and pushed off, stroking her way to the light beaming through the water at the surface, breaking into the air with a gasp, drawing breaths in gulps, then swam slowly to the shore, exhausted, pulling herself out onto the muddy bank and finally for a glorious moment of quiet, just lay there oblivious to nothing more than the pure beauty of solid earth and the sound of her heart beating upon it.

After catching her breath she pulled the tangled wet hair away from her face, and looked up at the waterfall she's just gone over.

"Well, that was lucky," she whispered.

She gathered herself into a sitting position, then tried to stand up and winced in pain.

"Not so lucky, ow."

She turned her ankle. This type of injury has happened before in her action packed life. Hopefully it was just a sprain. In the adrenaline rush of flying through the air a few times then getting dragged over a waterfall, she couldn't recall the exact moment that it happened. It wasn't black and blue yet, but felt like it was on the way. She started to take her shoe off, then thought better of it.

"I might never get it back on if it swells up."

15.

Grant decided to wait at the waterfall for five minutes to let her cool off, sitting on a nice dry flat rock eating a granola bar. He gazed at the list of ingredients on the package. Whole grain oats, sugar, oil, rice flour, blah, blah, blah.

Then came the warning disclaimer that it may contain soy which may in turn contain peanut ingredients, more blah, blah. He shook his giant bald head and chuckled. He could eat anything. One time at a party when he was a lot younger and trying to impress a bunch of chicks, he grabbed a giant cockroach that was crawling near a ceiling light, all the girls screamed until he tore off its head and ate it, crunching its wings with smacking lips and opening his mouth to show them the mashed up result before swallowing it whole. One of them fainted at the sight and the rest of them ran away. That got him some extra street cred up through middle school. Most people could eat almost anything, but just wanted to have an excuse to seem special, when in reality everyone was just an animal with clothes.

The only thing he would never, ever eat was a rat, or a bat, because they were both basically the same dirty creature, only one had wings.

He looked at his watch again to confirm. Five minutes. That's the amount of time that it takes a person to cool off from being angry. It's the amount of time he'd always been sent to time out when he was a kid, and they taught it in his anger management classes through the years. It should be enough time, he reasoned, for the big star to cool off at the boat, then he could take her back down for the rest of the film shoot.

He'd play the strong silent type again, apologize for being out of line, tell her it wouldn't happen again, and then ignore her.

He sat up, brushed off the crumbs, then started back down the trail. He got to the fork in the trail and went down the left side. When he got to the boat she was nowhere to be seen. He called out gently at first, then louder till the birds in the trees all flew off in fear. He went half-way back up the trail yelling her name till the veins stood out on the side of his neck.

"What the heck, I don't need this BS." He cursed, then snapped his fingers with an idea.

"She probably caught a ride on a kayak from another tour. I'll just go back down river, finish the photo shoot and be done with them. They can't fire me, I've got the only ski boat on the river this afternoon and they have a schedule to stick to. That producer is more concerned with his budget than anything else."

16.

Tom was in the shade, repairing the bottom of one the kayaks with a hole in it. These things happen when you're on a river that has rocks. He pried out the chewing gum he'd used as an emergency stop-gap up the river, and roughed up the hole with sandpaper. Then he mixed up some two part epoxy on a piece of cardboard, spread it over the hole with a small putty knife, then pressed it into the hole with a clear piece of plastic, and pulled it into the sun to cure.

"Twenty minutes to cure, and it'll be good as new."

Kanui was sitting on a beach chair, yawning.

"Tired," he said, rubbing his eyes.

"So take a nap," said Tom.

"Crazy. Soon as I close my eyes some nut on a water ski is gonna soak me." He laughed. "Hey you gotta admit it was pretty funny how Ashley Pepper sprayed you."

"Yeah, real funny," said Tom without a trace of humor.

"Man, if only I could have gotten a picture of it, we could've sold it to a magazine. You know, like the pepperoni guys."

Tom turned his deadpan face towards

Kanui.

"You mean the paparazzi guys?"

"Yeah whatever, those guys."

"Oh well, timing's everything. Knowing that wahine, maybe you'll have another chance. Get your camera ready."

"Hey check it out," said Kanui, sitting straight up in his chair, pointing up the river bank. "Grant's getting grilled."

The producer was in a heated conversation with Grant. Both their voices suddenly got so loud that half the park could hear what was being said. The camera men and grips were all standing around watching the action.

"What do you mean you can't find her?" shouted the producer.

"She must have taken the wrong trail on the way down from the waterfall."

"HELLO! You're the tour GUIDE! As in, you GUIDE her where to go!"

"She took off on her own! Said she wanted some time alone!"

"She doesn't know the terrain, you do. You shouldn't have let her out of your sight!"

"Well, if you ask me she's pretty hard headed. You of all people should know that."

"What do you mean by that?"

"You shouldn't have let her leave the set."

"I thought she was in GOOD HANDS!"

"She's probably real close to the trail. You can't get too far in that jungle."

"Not only is my star missing, but I've got a whole film crew getting paid to sit around on their rear ends."

"Hey it wasn't my idea for them to take an hour and a half break."

"Union rules."

"It was HER idea to go to the waterfall. I wash my hands of the whole thing. We're gonna need help," said Grant finally. "Let's get the whole film crew up there to help us look for her. Load them in the boat and we'll drive up there."

"You're fired," said the producer. He pulled out his phone and dialed 911.

Just a few minutes went by till a couple of sirens could be heard heading to the river, and within half an hour, an avalanche of attention poured out onto the scene, getting bigger and bigger as the minutes piled up.

Two police cars pulled up next to Grant's tent followed by a fire truck and rescue vehicle with yellow surfboards, then the lifeguard truck with the jet ski.

A rescue boat was being launched into the river, while a red fire department helicopter flew overhead, heading upstream. A uniformed policeman was interviewing Grant while writing on a tablet. A fireman stood nearby talking into a radio. The rescue boat headed up the river carrying half a dozen firemen carrying ropes and a liter, while a crowd gathered around the whole scene.

"Why don't you go check it out," said Tom. "See if you can find out what's happening."

Kanui walked back from the crowd scene a few minutes later shaking his head, while Tom was busy repairing another boat, unconcerned with the commotion.

"Holy cow," said Kanui. "They lost Ashley."

Tom didn't even look up from the work he was doing.

"So what's the story."

"Well, from what I could overhear, Grant took her up to the waterfall for a quick look while the film crew had their lunch break. She decided she wanted to hike back to the boat on her own, and he let her. When Grant came back down she was nowhere to be found, and he backtracked to the waterfall but still couldn't find her. They think she took a side trail by mistake, and now she's lost. Grant's a knuckle head. She could be anywhere by now."

Tom shrugged his shoulders.

"Those guys know what they're doing. They'll find her."

"Well anyways," said Kanui. "We're done for the day. They closed the waterfall area to conduct the search. No more tours are allowed up there. You want to pack it up and head out?"

Tom paused for a moment to think.

"You know I'd like to hang out for a while, see what happens."

"Well, if it's okay with you, I'll gonna head home, it's Constantina's birthday."

"You better not be late for that. Think you can catch a ride?"

"You kidding me? No problem here, this Portagee will catch a ride in two shakes."

"So what'd you get her for a present?

"Jade earrings. That should make her happy."

"Isn't jade from China?"

"Yeah why?

"I don't know, every time I think of China now, I think about Attila the Hun. Maybe the jade will bring a little of the Hun out in her."

Kanui sat still for a moment.

"Hey, don't joke around. I didn't even think about that." Then he cracked a wry smile. "Anyways, when she finds out Ashley Pepper is lost in a mosquito filled jungle I probably won't even need a present. See you tomorrow?"

"Seven AM..." Tom said, but Kanui finished his sentence.

"...on the dot."

Tom hefted the kayaks to the truck, loaded them into the trailer and tied them down. His personal kayak was still down by the river, waiting.

Deep in the valley, the sound of the search helicopter's engine, the thumping of the rotor blades increased and decreased in volume as it dipped in and out of the crevasses lining the edge of the river.

His brow furrowed as he came to a decision that made him shake his head. He took a backpack from the rear seat of the truck and checked the supplies. It was always ready to go on a moment's notice. Coffee, granola bars, water purifier, sterno, flashlight, flotation devices, and a tent. The minimal essentials. As an afterthought and against his normal procedure, he took the cell phone from his pocket, sealed in two separate zip lock baggies and put it in a back pocket of the pack.

Twenty minutes later he was paddling up the river towards the drop zone for the waterfall hike. Muttering to himself.

"What are you doing Tom?"

He turned down the side waterway, paddled to the end and pulled the kayak up onto the river bank. All the day tour kayaks are gone, and the bank was empty except for the fire department's rescue skiff. A lone fire fighter is on the river bank, talking into a walkie talkie. He put it to the side while watching Tom approach. The lettering on his helmet read; KANE.

"Hey Tom."

"Any word yet Kane?"

"None yet. We closed the area around the waterfall while we do a sweep. Don't want any lookie-loos getting in the way."

"Lots of nooks and crannies up there. Plenty of spots to get stuck. Jungle so thick you can't see the sky."

Kane's face lightened up.

"We sure had a lot of fun when we were kids, remember? A big gang of us in grade school and junior high. Hiking around in our camo gear with our BB guns, playing army commandos. Sometimes we'd camp out overnight, one time we almost made it for a week. Man, those were the days."

Tom nodded.

"Yeah."

"Most everyone stopped going, drifted away, got regular jobs, married with kids." said Kane. "Except for you. Somehow you found a way to keep coming up here, and get paid to do it."

"Not paid much. Hey I heard you made chief."

Kane laughed.

"Assistant chief. Half the pay for twice the load as the big cheese gets."

"I'll tell you what though," said Tom. "When I heard the news it put a little hop in my step. I know you've been trying for a long time. They kept putting you on the bottom shelf, but you never gave up. It's good to see one of our old crew make it to the big time."

Kane looked around at the jungle.

"Most of my work these days is behind a desk. I forgot how nice it was up here."

"It's God's country."

"Sure seems like it," said Kane.

"Listen," said Tom. "I was thinking about lending a hand maybe, and take a look around. No big deal. I won't get in anyone's way. If that's okay."

"Are you kidding me? It's fine with me. More than fine. This is kind of like your backyard anyways. I'll get on the horn and let everyone know."

They bumped knuckles, Tom shouldered the backpack and started to head up the trail.

"Hey Tom!" shouted Kane, stopping him cold.

"Yeah?"

"Don't get lost."

"Yeah right."

They both chuckled, then Tom continued up the trail out of sight.

Kane put the walkie talkie next to his face again, clicking on the button.

"This is command one. Be advised that Tom O'Malley is heading into the search area to look around. Over."

17.

Emmerete Peele sat in the gleaming office at the top corner of the production building on Wilshire Boulevard. Multiple piles of paper half a foot tall sat on his desk waiting for him to scan through them.

Stacks of screenplays that his team thought might be worth a look. They could all wait. It was nearly the weekend, and even though weekends usually just meant more work, this one was different. They'd finished principal filming for Ashley Pepper's new film two weeks early, which meant that they were under budget for once. And that was a cause for celebration. Maybe a bottle of wine down at the beach house at Malibu, a small dinner with just he and the wife, cooked by their personal chef to perfection. He told himself that he deserved it. The editing team had the ball in their court now, and it would be a few days before he'd need to check in on them to see the progress. This was the time to let the director and the editor have some space. Crowding the talent when they were trying to craft a masterpiece usually never worked. His director was busy molding, carving, shaping ninety minutes of film from three thousand minutes of out-takes.

During production Emmerette was a lion of sorts, roaring when needed which was often.

Planning for a multi-million dollar film was utmost. Plan to the exact, and then execute that plan exactly. Everything was in the process. If you planned to perfection, you should be able to execute the plan to perfection. Unfortunately it usually never worked out that way. There were always the little bastardly unplannable mis-haps, snafus, equipment malfunctions, illnesses, injuries, permit oversights, legal hurdles. Theirs was a business of large fragile egos, and sometimes peoples feeling's got hurt and needed a mental massage, or the exact perfect diet to make them happy. They were sore, they didn't sleep right, someone made them angry or sad. Often times they came to work hung over. There were disagreements of language, scripting issues, stunts that looked easy on paper but proved in real life to be nearly impossible.

Those were sometimes the hardest nut of all to crack. Ashley's films always had a high amount of drama since they used a large percentage of up close and personal stunts to take advantage of her exceptional athletic shape. She wasn't built to hide behind props, or lavish wardrobes, her image was made to flaunt in the highest visibility they could manage on a giant silver screen in HD. That's where the money was. Give the audience what they wanted, and they wanted skin.

Finally he could see the light at the end of

the tunnel of a project that started out much like what was sitting on the corner of his desk right now, squashed in the middle of a stack of screenplays written by an endless horde of hopeful, starving writers. A little gem of a story that they'd found, a gem in the rough that they managed to bend and cut and stich together into a crafty little film that fit the style that Miss Ashley's wealthy retainers demanded.

She was under contract for one more film after this one was complete, and then let the fun begin. If the next two turned out to be blockbusters like the last one, she wouldn't be an under budget movie star any longer, she'd be able to command a fortune for any subsequent films.

She would in essence become a budget buster, if they could even find a story to fit her.

The landline on his desk rang, a simple two bell ring, he stared at the offending black oblique cradled safely and thought twice about answering it before picking it up.

"Hello."

"Emmerette?"

"Yes, can I help you?"

"This is Stuart, are you sitting down?"

"Yes, why?"

"Ashley's missing."

"What do you mean missing. C'mon man fill in the blanks, she's been missing before."

"She's in Hawaii for a photo shoot..."

"Yes, yes I know, come out with it."

"Well, apparently she went for a hike in between takes, to some waterfall, probably took a wrong turn on the trail, and is lost in the jungle. We hope."

"What do you mean we hope."

"Well, there's water everywhere, and well, we just hope she's only lost in the jungle and nothing worse."

"Ashley?" He scoffed loudly. "That girl was practically born in the water. I think her mother gave birth to her in one of those birthing pools. Maybe even one that has dolphins in it as agile as she is."

Emmerette's mind was spinning faster than a roulette wheel in Vegas. Where would the wheel stop. The options were both frightening and exhilarating. The old adage that any publicity was good publicity was true with the humans that were currently running around on the planet. They wanted action, good or bad, happy or sad.

If they found Ashley too quickly, it would be a ho-hummer of a story, fit for the back page. If they couldn't find her for a while it enhanced the story line and brought more eyes to the table worldwide. If she was injured or... He hesitated at that thought, not sure he wanted to go there. If she didn't survive, that would make it a story bigger than the entire world could handle, for a short amount time anyways, until the next new big story came along.

It wouldn't be the first time that an actor died before their movie hit the big screen.

Four options. Actually five. What if they never found her. He shook off that thought, the worst of all. His whirling mind came quickly back to the present.

"Okay Stuart, what's the rest of the story?"

"She went to the waterfall with one of the guys on the set, the boat driver. He tried to kiss her, she stomped off, he followed but couldn't find her, or so he says. They mobilized all the rescue assets they have on the island, helicopters, firefighters, bloodhounds, they even called in a military chopper from Oahu with thermal heat sensors. One of the problems with that unfortunately is there's a lot of feral pigs out in the jungle, from what they tell me."

Ashley Pepper, lost in the jungle with feral pigs running wild. She's probably covered in mud. Half-naked. Scratched by giant ferns. Hair tussled. She's frightened and alone.

Emmerette stroked his mustache, deep in thought.

"Oh, and there's one other thing," said Stuart.

"What's that?"

"There's a tropical storm off the coast that just turned into a hurricane and it's headed straight for the island."

"Astounding," said Emmerette. You couldn't make this stuff up. He looked at the stack of screenplays, shook his finger and laughed at them. Posers. "Say Stuart, what time is it over there?"

There was a pause on the other end, then;

"Four thirty, it doesn't get dark for another couple of hours. They still have time to find her."

"Oh, I'm not worried about Ashley. That girl

is about as tough as they come. Keep me updated."

He hung up the phone. The bottle of wine and dinner in Malibu would have to wait for another day. Now was the time to make big money. A force multiplier had miraculously dropped into their lap. He picked up the phone and dialed another number. The voice on the other end was just as business-like as Emmerette had been to Stuart.

"Peach here, how can I help you."

Jim Peach, head of marketing for the studio was also just about to head out of his office, but he had bigger plans than a little dinner in Malibu. The Lakers Clippers game was in an hour and he had fifth row seats mid court. They were the best seats in the house. Forget about sitting right next to the courtside, having all those giant dudes with their sweat and saliva flying on you as they raced past, or maybe crashing into you, falling right on top of you with bone crushing weight while they scrambled for a loose ball. It'd be like having a giraffe fall on you for crying out loud. He liked getting close to the action, but not that close. Having a sweaty six foot ten, three hundred pound Goliath plow into you at full speed, maybe two or three of them at once was not his idea of a fun time.

"This is Emmerette."

"Boss. What can I do for you."

"Mobilize your team. Have you heard about Ashley?"

Peach held his breath.

"Holy cow, what happened."

"Nothing yet. She disappeared in Hawaii, got lost in the jungle."

Peach was suddenly unimpressed. Lakers Clippers, hello.

"That's it? What's the angle?"

"Mud, feral pigs, hurricane."

"Hmmm. Let me think about this. How long ago did it happen?"

"About half an hour. I don't think it hit the wire yet."

"Maybe they'll find her. Last thing we want is to come across as crazy lunatics shouting that the sky is falling or cry wolf and be accused as frantic nellies."

"I agree."

"We're a top tier film production company. We remain calm and poised during any crisis. I'll call one contact at TMZ and let them know it's all under control, nothing to worry about, we have full confidence that the local authorities will find her safe and sound. The more I underplay it, the more they'll suspect that something is wrong. I'll let them sound the alarm."

"As always I rely on your wisdom," said Emmerette.

"Then we'll get a press release ready once we have all the facts and get it out to all the newspaper, radio, and TV news shows. Don't worry, I'm on it right this minute."

"Okay give me an update when you have it," said Emmerette and hung up the phone.

Peach looked at his computer screen as the

phone call ended. He jumped on the internet and pulled up a weather site of the Hawaiian islands, an animated satellite map showing a round circle of clouds five hundred miles wide with a hole in the middle creeping towards the chain.

"So there is a hurricane heading that way," he muttered. "I had no idea."

His heart skipped a beat with the sudden implication. Getting lost in the jungle in Hawaii wasn't usually a big problem, there were no predators, or snakes. The land area was small, a search crew should be able to find even the most entrenched person with the technology they had these days. Feral pigs were a nuisance but not dangerous. But a hurricane. Those could kill people, especially those who were caught out in the open. Flying branches, torrential floods.

He stood up out of his chair and headed for the door, checking his watch. Fifty minutes to game time. He could still stop and pick up a sandwich and make it on time. The best thing about marketing is that you didn't have to be sitting at a desk to work. All you needed was a phone.

He dialed quick as he waited for elevator, the phone rang twice.

"Dan here."

"This is Peach. I have a code red for you. I need a precise and concise absolutely bullet proof press release pronto."

"What's up?"

"Ashley Pepper lost in the jungle in Hawaii.

Feral pigs, hurricane. Get Smiley and find all the details, who what why where when, roll it into a draft and get it to me as soon as you can to review. I'm heading to the game."

"Lakers Clippers?"

"Is there any other game in town that you know of? Is there any other game in the country? The world?"

"I tried to get tickets but it's sold out."

"That's right and I got the last one. Besides you have to work. So get on the horn to Smiley and get those details."

Peach almost thought he could hear the sound of a defeated sigh on the other end.

"Dan, are you still there?"

"Yeah I'm still here, we'll get on it. I want to find out what going on. Now I'm really worried about Ashley."

"Don't worry, there's no worrying in our business, just get the facts."

Peach pressed the red button to end the call as the elevator reached the lobby.

He strolled out the front door, hailed a cab, then got right back on the phone, pulled up his contacts, scrolled down the giant list, and pressed his finger on the little pixie face that appeared.

Her voice was a pleasant mix of syrupy southern charm and elegant Midwestern country girl that perfectly matched the face on his phone.

"Why Jim Peach, to what do I have to thank for this splendid honor."

He was quick and to the point.

"Georgette, I have a scoop for you, but I don't want you to worry too much about it. Ashley's going to be fine, we have all the confidence in the world that the local authorities in Hawaii are doing everything they can to find her and we should have a successful outcome to report soon."

Word for word, just as he'd planned it.

He could hear giggling on the other end, that turned into outright laughter before she finally came back, sober again.

"That's so cute of you, thinking you were going to give me a scoop. You do know who you're talking to darling, don't you? I have eyes and ears everywhere..."

He could imagine her triumphant smile as she spoke.

"...In fact we have one of our ace reporters heading to the scene as we speak."

"From L.A.?"

"No, from Honolulu. It would take too long to fly someone from L.A. to Hawaii. We were actually very lucky to have someone so near. She was on vacation in Waikiki and agreed to fly over to cover the action. It's only a half hour flight you know. Actually she begged us to put her on the story. And who wouldn't, in our business anyways. Ashley Pepper attracts quite a following."

Peach smiled. Yes she did. He loved giving Georgette a hard time, almost as much as she loved giving it back to him.

"So it sounds like you have the on-camera talent right around the corner. You got that angle covered. What about the actual camera itself. You know the little thing that records the action and sends it to the watching device."

She wanted to tell him that the only little thing was between his legs, but she kept it civil.

"Don't worry about us sugar, we have that all sewn up. We have a local crew from Honolulu on the way. They should be there any minute."

"Union crew?"

"Of course. Why do you ask?"

"I don't know. A story this big, I would have thought you'd have your own crew headed there. No matter what it took."

Her voice maintained its high sugar content.

"But I thought you said it wasn't a big deal, nothing to worry about?"

"Oh not for us Georgette. We're not worried. But for you... I don't know, I'd hate to have the local film crew you hired turn out to be, how do I put it... less than average. And I'd really hate to have the nationwide, no we'd better make that worldwide viral clips come from your rivals. Well I have to run sugar lips. My stop's coming up and I have to pay for the cab. Bye."

He pressed the red button. Check that box. He could almost imagine her squirming at not getting in the last word.

Georgette looked at the phone that suddenly went blank. How rude. He hung up on her.

She scrolled through her phone, found the face she was looking for with the pony tail and goofy grin, then punched that face with a finely manicured nail.

"C'mon Paul, pick up, pick up."

Five rings later, just before it went to voicemail a young energetic voice came on the phone.

"Hi Georgette, I was going to call you. We have the footage you wanted from this morning. The guy's in editing are running through it."

"Forget about that. I need you to find Max and get on a plane to Hawaii right now."

"What?" His voice trembled.

"Ashley Pepper is lost in some damn jungle over there and I don't want that bitch Louise to get a better shot than us. I just know that she's sending her best crew. Get all your gear, double up on everything, no make that triple, it's like you're going to some foreign country for crying out loud. I'll call the airlines and get you the next flight out and I'll text you the boarding passes."

"Okay," he said sullenly.

The phone went blank as she hung up on the other end. He looked at it with remorse, then turned to Max who was standing next to him outside the Staples Center. They were waiting in line to get through the doors. Max was wearing a Lakers shirt, while Paul was wearing a Clippers shirt. The two friends were fierce rivals and had been looking forward to this game all year. Heckling each other every day.

They bought the tickets the moment they went on sale, the very moment that the seasons schedule was announced. You couldn't get your hands on a ticket now unless your first name was Magic.

"I don't like the look on your face," said Max. "What's up?"

"Duty calls. We have to go to Hawaii."

"Tomorrow right? Or after the game," said Max hopefully.

"Now, like right now."

Paul held up his ticket in his right hand, without saying a word. Held it high and started walking out from the entrance towards the jackals waiting on the fringes. Max hung his head following suit, ticket in the air. The world as far as he was concerned, had just come to an end. Three people raced towards them.

"Two hundred each," Paul said simply. "Tenth row, mid court."

"I'll give you five hundred for both," said one burly guy who gave the other two hopeful ticket buyers a dirty look. They backed off and the exchange was made.

Max however, wouldn't let go of the ticket, his fingers were locked tight with some sort of strange instantaneous arthritis, and it took a couple of tries for the burly guy to wrestle it away from him. He finally won out though, as people crowded around to see if there was going to be a fight. A large security officer began to make his way through the crowd before both men finally parted. Max with a scowl the size of L.A. on his face. The burley guy immediately put the two tickets back in the air, back on the market.

"Don't worry," said Paul as they made their way to the parking lot. "There's always next year."

18.

As Tom hiked along the trail, thick jungle on all sides, the search helicopter flew directly overhead, so low that it was flattening the trees as it went, heading to another portion of the valley. He got to the clearing at the waterfall and looked around. One firefighter was standing by the pool searching the surrounding cliffs with a pair of binoculars.

Tom headed back down the trail, searching the sides for clues. It was a muddy mess, hundreds of shoe prints. He got to a small fork in the trail and took the right side heading up to the top of the ridge. Here, there were just a few footprints, some heavy boots, and others small and indistinguishable, even some that looked like they could be pig hooves.

Two firefighters were coming back down the trail laden down with climbing ropes. They shook their heads as they saw him.

"We went all the way to the top Tom. There's no sign of her. We're going to head down and search the ridge on the other side of the stream."

"Alright, well maybe I'll just give it another look. I haven't been up this way in a while."

"Suit yourself."

He trudged up the trail while the firefighters headed back down.

The vegetation in this area was mostly lantana fern, with a few patches of cats claw, the invasive sprawling shrub with thorns that grow along and at the ends of stems and leaves, grabbing at you like an angry cat. If a single thorn snags you and you're not careful and try to wriggle away from it, the branch bends towards you and more thorns entangle you.

"Popoki," he said, Hawaiian for cat. "Stay away from me."

He picked up a stick and used it to fend off the drooping branches and slide by them. On the ground at the other side of the bramble bush was a broken branch. A single strand of hair was wrapped in a curved claw at the end. Long and black. Could just be a coincidence. A strand of hair could look fresh for months. Although the broken end of the branch looked like it could be as fresh as a week or less.

He kept hiking up onto the ridge and came to the place where you can just barely see the little waterfall down in the valley. Waterfall number five they called it. The helicopter must have flown right over this area since the ferns looked like they were all flattened down from the windstorm.

Then he saw it, a little space in the ferns, barely noticeable to the eye. He pushed into the thicket and there, barely noticeable was a tiny little trail leading deeper into the brush.

"Could be a goat, or a pig."

He studied the ground as he moved forward.

"No prints, hard to tell what kind of animal."

He pushed forward, the going getting tougher, spiky lantana pulling at his arms, but thankfully no popiki.

"This is crazy," he muttered to himself. "There's no way a pampered little princess starlet is going off the trail into this stuff."

Then he saw it. The ground here was muddy and there plain as day was a shoe print.

"Well what do you know. Sure aint a goat or a pig, unless they're wearing a size seven."

He put his shoe next to it for comparison.

"Small enough for a girls maybe, could just be a kid."

He continued on, pushing through the ferns as they got thicker, till he came to the edge of the valley. Experience in these situations taught him not to push through a wall of ferns unless he was sure what was on the other side, and in this case it seemed like air.

Sure enough as he gingerly parted the matted green branches he was looking over the edge of a muddy cliff that ended in a stream far below.

"Looks like something slid down that hill. I better call the boys, have the chopper come take a look down there."

He had a bad feeling in the pit of his stomach. Maybe she fell down the hill and was at the bottom in bad shape.

With one eye on the muddy slope below his feet he started to take off the backpack to get to the cell phone. He was impatient. Tired from a long day and then somehow getting sucked up into looking for the spoiled one. The backpack snagged on a fern while the shoulder pad was still hooked onto his right elbow, he struggled to get the pack free, first his right foot slipped just a bit but enough to get his full attention, then while gaining balance on that side, overcompensated with his left which slipped in the opposite direction. Two feet splayed in different directions holding them motionless, both of them ready to slip completely at the slightest pressure, at an impasse, held in check by the backpack hooked onto the fern which made the tiniest sound of a snap, letting the back pack free.

Both feet slipped at once, he tried to skate his way back to an upright position, but there was no traction on the ground. Down onto his backside, sliding down the hill, he flailed at the sides of the mud hill trying to grab a branch but was going too fast, picking up speed, hitting the speed bump, up and over the berm, landing in the pool of water, his right foot shuddered straight down on a rock and his leg went numb, and came up sputtering. Blurry eyes looking up at the treacherous hill.

Underwater his feet were slipping on the rocks. His right foot suddenly useless. The current much stronger than he'd anticipated, quickly now, over a ledge, down onto the moss covered lava tube, flying through the air again and landed in the big pool below.

He came to the surface, gasping for air, struggling to the edge of the pond. Pulled himself onto a ledge of wet black rocks, looked up and saw a foot, followed that up to a pair of ankles, then long legs and an amused face.

Ashley Pepper was looking down at him, smiling.

"Fun ride isn't it?"

"What..." he was shaken and injured.

"I said it's a fun ride. I went on it too. Except I sprained my ankle and can't walk. Hey I remember you, from the river, you were paddling the kayak."

As he sat on the wet rocks, his mind returned.

"Yeah, I seem to remember a little spray in my face. Anyone ever tell you it's not safe to leave the trail?"

"I did not spray you on purpose, it was that idiot boat driver Grant. And you're one to talk, what are you doing off the trail?"

"Looking for you I guess. Half the fire department is out looking for you."

Tom grimaced, and tried to get out of the water, holding his right leg.

"Oh my gosh, are you all right." Her playful animosity gone, she grabbed for his hand and helped him out of the water.

"Feels like it's broke. Maybe it's just a sprain though, I don't know."

"Well aren't we a pair. Look I'm sorry we got off on the wrong foot so to speak. My name is Ashley Pepper."

"Yeah, I know. I'm Tom O'Malley."

"O'Malley, an Irishman."

"In this case I'm an 'I Wish' man. As in I

wish I didn't slide down that hill. I knew you were trouble the moment I saw you. What the heck are you doing way out here? Do you know the kind of mess we're in? We're gonna have to get air lifted out of here."

Her eyes narrowed, blood boiling.

"Hey, I didn't ask you to come looking for me."

They had a silent truce for a moment, then Ashley opened up.

"That gross Grant got a little grabby at the waterfall and I had to get away from him, fast. I must have taken the wrong turn, then I came to the edge of this valley and saw this most beautiful waterfall in the distance. I just wanted to sit by it for a minute."

"Well, you got your wish."

"Do the other searchers know where you are?"

"No, not really. I was just about to make the call when I slid down that damn hill."

He pulled his backpack closer, opened up the back pocket pulling out the cell phone wrapped in the zip baggies, opened them up to find a dripping wet smashed phone.

"Great," whispered Tom. "That's a hundred bucks..."

He looked at her frowning, although he already knew the answer, since if she did have a phone she would have used it by now, still the question had to be asked.

"Do you have a phone?"

She smiled.

"Sure do."

She reached behind her and held up a phone with a cracked faceplate, water still dripping from it.

"Now what?" She asked.

He shook his and sighed, thinking hard.

"Remember earlier when I said we were in big trouble? Well it just got worse. We're not going to get out of here anytime soon. Add to that it's gonna get dark pretty quick as deep in the valley as we are." He looked around, considering the options. "We'd better get ready. Don't worry, whenever I come up to the valleys, I always come prepared."

He limped over to a level spot and began to unload the backpack.

"Give me a hand setting up this tent."

She didn't answer him, just sat there looking at him with a blank face.

"Well?" He asked.

"Well what?" Her face didn't change.

"Are you going to help with the tent, or not?"

"Have you ever heard of the word 'please'?"

He sighed and said a small silent prayer to help him keep his composure in the face of adversity. "Please help me with the tent that will save your life."

Twenty minutes later, his ankle throbbing in pain and unable to stand, Tom was sitting on the side giving the final instructions to Ashley.

"Okay, now thread that support through the ring. Not that ring, the other ring!"

"Are you always this grumpy?"

"Only when I'm stuck in the wilderness with a broken leg."

"My ankle is hurt too buddy, and it could be worse."

"How's that?"

"You could be alone with no one to help you set up this tent."

"Yeah, well okay, good point, just thread that support and let's get this done."

With the tent finally set up, Tom sat at the entrance tightening up the supports. Ashley sat nearby, eyes intently watching the waterfall. Intrigued by the everchanging liquid motion. Mesmerized.

He broke her out of her trance.

"Are you hungry?" he asked.

"Starving, but I'm used to it."

"What?"

"The camera puts an extra twenty pounds on you. I'm always on a diet."

"Doesn't sound like a lot of fun."

"It's not."

"Granola bar?"

He reached out a wrapped bar and she took it a genuine smile.

"Thank you, I could eat these all day."

"Well go easy on it, I only have a couple more."

"This has been my dream, to camp out next to a waterfall in Hawaii."

"Well don't get used to it, we're getting out of here tomorrow."

"I'm just going to lay here and listen to it all night."

"You do and the mosquitos will carry you off."

"There's mosquitos?"

"Millions. And they come out at night."

She looked suspiciously at the tent. For the first time, even after struggling and putting the dang thing up, she suddenly realized how tiny it was.

"That tent only looks big enough for one person."

Here we go, thought Tom.

"It's a two man tent."

"It's small."

"Well I'm sorry I forgot to pack the mansion sized tent."

"I don't' know," she said, sniffing the air. "I think I'll take my chances out here. How bad can it be?"

"Suit yourself."

He pulled himself into the tent, and zipped up the screen door.

"See you in the morning," he said.

"Some gentleman you are. A couple of little mosquitos won't hurt me."

As it slowly got darker, a mosquito buzzed by her ear. She swatted it away. Another buzzed by the other ear. Swat. She looked down at her leg in the fading light to see over a dozen blood suckers attached to it.

Tom heard the shriek, then the tent being frantically unzipped.

"Any mosquitos?"

"Very funny, just keep your hands to yourself buster."

"You won't have any trouble from me."

She had a hard time with the zipper.

"Well hurry up, don't let them in here!" he snapped

"I'm trying!"

He switched on the flashlight so he could see the progress. She finally pulled the zipper to the bottom, and flopped over onto the empty side of the tent. He double checked the zipper, and satisfied that it was secure laid back down.

"Here, you can have the backpack for a pillow, I have a poncho I can roll up."

"Thanks," she said and lay on her side looking away from him. Tom rolled the other way looking away from her.

They both kept their eyes open for a few moments. Nothing more needed to be said, they were stuck together and could feel the electric presence of each other's bodies.

Then it began to rain. Gently at first, and then a steady downpour. That sound plus the waterfall and the long drawn out day put a spell on them, and they both fell soundly asleep.

19.

Grant sat in the hard backed chair while looking across the table at the two detectives.

"I didn't do anything," he said simply. "You have to let me go."

"We're holding you for questioning," said the smaller of the two, the Portagee wearing the crisp pressed short sleeve black uniform, two bars on the lapel. The name tag above his left breast pocket read Lieutenant Andrade. He was the boss of the show, and make no mistake about it, his small stature didn't stand in the way of his enthusiasm for his job.

He probably weighed in at a buck fifty Grant reckoned, and could be thrown across the room like a sack of potatoes with enough running room. The other cop was a different story. He sat an arm's length from Andrade, spread out in his seat like a king on his throne. He really needed two chairs. Sergeant Chang read the name tag on the ruffled blue uniform of a beat cop. This was not a man to be trifled with. He was part Hawaiian, Chinese, Tongan. Maybe a little bit of Samoan for good measure. And he obviously liked to eat. His arms alone were the size of most normal human's legs. And even though he was super-sized, he had the tallowy elastic flow to his movements that gave you the impression that he could probably move pretty quick if he wanted.

There was no sure way to gauge his weight by looking at him, maybe it was two seventy five, maybe three fifty. One thing for sure, no one was going to throw this guy around. His face was round and semi-flat around the eye sockets. His nickname around the island was Pie face, and if you called him that in his presence, you'd damn well better be a good friend of his.

Grant was not, and held his tongue. Pie face, sergeant Chang that is, and Grant went *way* back. Chang was a year younger and grew up on the West side of the island, but they somehow found a way to tangle through sports in their younger days, and neither one of them ever forgot it. First was in Pee Wee football, then all the way through Mustang, and then High School. Grant was a pretty big boy too, and always seemed to get lined up on the other side of Chang who started out smaller in comparison, but that didn't last.

The first time they ever met they were probably just ten and eleven years old. Even back then Grant was a natural trash talker, and on game day when they saw each for the first time, neither one seemed to take a liking to the other. Chang was at center, while Grant lined up at nose tackle. They grimaced at each other through their facemasks. Tough guys.

"I'm gonna stomp your ass into a mud hole,"

said Grant with a snarl. And then did just that, bulldozing little Chang over and pile driving him into the turf.

That scene played out many times over the next few years until High school rolled along.

Grant was a sophomore and still bullrushing his opponents off the ball and was gunning for the school record for tackles. He hadn't seen Chang on the other side of the scrimmage line in a few years. And then Chang came back on the scene.

Over the past two years he'd put on over a hundred pounds and was the up and coming bruiser on the island. Even as a freshman he was a dominating presence. At first Grant didn't recognize him, then grinned at him through his face mask. 'Oh yeah', he thought to himself. Here was the kid he tortured over the years. So what if he looked a little larger. It wouldn't matter. After all he reckoned, the bigger they are the harder they fall.

"I see you're back for some more lessons," he mocked. "What'd you do with the other Chang, eat him?"

But Chang remained silent, gritting his teeth until he hiked the ball, then charged forward at Grant, standing him up like a grizzly bear in full attack mode, pushing him straight back ten feet till he cartwheeled him over onto his helmet. Then Chang stood over him for a moment looking down at him, before walking back to the huddle, scuffing some dirt backwards from his cleats as he went.

For the next three years Grant could not

solve the puzzle of how to get around the sudden monster from the West side. And he wasn't alone. No one else on their team, or on either one of the three teams on the island could find a way around the big guy. The West side high school football team rolled behind their big guy, and was the island champs for two years in a row, and then on the third year, when Chang was a Junior and Grant was a senior they met one last time in the Championship game.

It was just the first quarter, the West side was leading by a touchdown, seven to nothing, and driving from mid-field for another score with punishing runs behind their big center, when Grant accidently stepped on Chang's right hand while everyone was down in the pile, breaking it. That resulted in a bench clearing brawl that saw multiple players ejected, but the damage was done. The stone pillar in the middle was gone, and the East side high school team rolled onto victory, and even though Grant had to watch from the sidelines, being ejected from the game, he smiled at the sweetness of it all. Winning was everything.

"You waived your Miranda rights, and declined to have your lawyer present," continued Lieutenant Andrade. "This interview is being taped, so anything you say can and will be used against you in a court of law. I just want to make that doubly clear Grant."

"I don't need a lawyer, I didn't do anything wrong."

"We have two witnesses who saw you try to

kiss Ashley, she shoved you away from her, and then after a brief verbal exchange which they could not hear, she walked down the trail towards the river. A few minutes later you followed her, and that's the last they saw of either one of you. In fact, that's the last time anyone saw Ashley."

"Sure I leaned over to kiss her. I thought she wanted me to. There's no law against that is there?"

Andrade frowned and sighed. The word idiot came to mind. "Of course it's against the law. It's sexual assault."

"For a kiss that didn't even happen?" Grant was incredulous.

"Did she give you permission to kiss her?"

"Well no, but she implied it."

Andrade shook his head. "Implied it."

"Look," said Grant. "She practically begged me to take her up to the waterfall. C'mon guys, we all know what that means. A girl asks you to take her to the waterfall is code for she wants to get naked with you."

Andrade kept his face steady. If Grant wanted to keep digging a hole for himself, why not let him. "Continue," he said.

Grant looked from Andrade to Chang then back again, and stopped himself. He almost started to smile, but also kept his facial expression neutral. He recognized a trap.

"Look," he said. "She asked me to take her to the waterfall. Alone. On this island, growing up, we all know that means the green light."

"She's not from this island."

"Okay, so I made a simple mistake. It was a misunderstanding between two individuals. I didn't touch her, I didn't assault her, our lips never met. I leaned over to kiss her, she refused my advances and walked away. That's the last I ever saw of her. No matter what the witnesses who saw me try to kiss her say, our lips never met."

Chang made a slight movement, shifting in his chair, and for a man that size, a slight movement was like the earth changing orbits.

He looked down at his right hand, the size of a baseball mitt, the one that was broken on that fateful championship game day long ago. He flexed it ever so slightly, like a bear warming up after a long winter's nap and then spoke. His voice was calm and light, belying the inner beast. His chair creaked slightly under his weight. He looked up from his hand, then focused his eyes on Grant as he spoke simply.

"You better hope we find her alive."

20.

Dawn creeped slowly into the valley. Song birds warbled in the trees surrounding the little cove, while the waterfall gently gushed into the pool.

In the tent, Ashley was curled on her side with her head nestled gently on Tom's shoulder.

He woke up, saw her there and smiled wryly. He slept soundly through the night and hadn't even noticed that she had snuggled up practically on top of him till this very moment. He closed his eyes and pretended to snore. Not a loud snore, just a light one, enough to get her attention without being obvious.

She woke up groggily from another world, another universe. Blackness, and nothingness turning to light and harmonic vibrations. There was an obnoxious sound right next to her ear. She heard that sound or something like it, somewhere long ago in her past. There it was again, a light rasping sound streaming in to one ear that was exposed to the air, while from the other that was somehow flat on a soft surface, was the sound of a heartbeat. Her eyes snapped wide, suddenly realizing where her head was resting, carefully lifted it off without disturbing the sleeping bear, and quietly rolled back onto her side of the tent, biting her lip.

Off in the distance, the faint thump of a helicopter rotor blade echoed into the valley.

She sat up abruptly.

"Do you hear that?"

"Helicopter," said Tom.

They both scrambled for the screen door zipper. Ashley got her hand on it first.

"Easy with it," said Tom. "Easy! Don't force it!"

"It's stuck!"

"Yeah, because you're forcing it, let go!"

They're wrestling over the zipper. Tom finally gets control.

"Argghhhh!" yells Ashley and lets go of it. Tom now has both hands on it, trying to maneuver it open.

The sound of the helicopter is louder now, and is right over their heads, noise deafening.

"We're saved!" shouted Ashley. "Hurry up!"

"You got the teeth bent."

Finally by zipping it forward then backwards he's able to get it moving again, quickly opening it with one fluid motion. Ashley bolted out of the door waving as the helicopter flew off down the valley. It was so close she could just about hit the tail with a rock, yelling at the top of her lungs.

"We're over here! Over here! Hey! Hey! Hey!"

But it was too late, the chopper slowly disappeared out of sight down the little valley, and around a bend in the stream.

"What the heck is wrong with them?" she fumed. "They were so close we could have jumped up into the pilot's seat. Why couldn't they see us?'

Then she looked over at the tent.

"A camouflage tent, great. And why do you have a camo tent?"

Tom has given up and lays back down in the tent.

"Old habit."

Ashley was waiting for an answer with her hands on her hips.

"I like to go camping," he said simply.

She had an angry puzzled look on her face so he continued.

"The state charges camping fees, and I don't want to pay them. So I blend in.

"So you're an illegal camper? That's how you get your thills?"

"What's illegal to some people is freedom, to others. They want to charge me money to go camping in the wilderness? I say the heck with 'em. This is God's country. It should be illegal for them to charge money to be out here."

"So you like to blend in?"

"Love it."

"Well it sure worked this time genius."

"Are you always this cranky in the morning?"

She sat down and rubbed her ankle.

"Only when I'm lost in the wilderness with a twisted ankle, a camouflage tent, and no coffee."

"I have coffee."

She brightened up.

"And we're not lost. I know exactly where we are and how we're going to get out of here. I've been here before. A long time ago. Although I didn't get here quite the same way as I did yesterday."

He dug into the backpack and pulled out a pot.

"Why don't you go fill this up with water and I'll make you some coffee."

Five short minutes later the pot was sitting on four flat rock above a can of sterno. When the water started to boil, he poured two tiny sleeves of coffee into the pot.

"Instant coffee."

He poured the coffee into a cup and handed it to her.

"What about you?" she asked.

"I'll wait for the pot to cool off a bit and drink it straight from there."

She blew on the surface of the hot black water, took a sip of the steaming drink and closed her eyes.

"This tastes better than the best cup of latte at the Ritz."

"The setting probably has something to do with it."

"Restaurants call it the presentation," she said.

How's the ankle?" he asked.

"It hurts, but not as bad as yesterday. I can walk but I don't know about hiking up that hill., and then hiking out. Do you think the helicopter will come back?"

"I don't know. One thing I do know for sure is I'm not definitely not hiking out of here."

"You think it's broken," she asked.

"Naw, it's probably just a sprain, or torn ligaments. In the shape I'm in it would take me two days to hike back up that ridge."

"So now what, do we wait here?"

"I imagine they'll probably have a pretty big search crew out looking for you. The problem is that they've already scanned this valley with a helicopter and they might not come back this way again for a long time. If ever."

"So we're going to have to try to hike out."

"There's another way. We'll float out."

"Float out?"

"You see, this stream ends up back at the river. It winds around a lot before it gets there, but it does eventually get there. We'll have to navigate a couple of steep parts on the ways, but it'll be a whole lot easier than trying to hike out in the condition we're in."

"Float out. Are you planning on making a raft out of sticks, or do you have an inflatable dingy in that backpack?"

"Funny you should ask."

He reached into the backpack and pulled out two little square plastic wrapped packages. He took one out of the wrapping, unfolded it and started to blow it up. It was colorful, with rainbows and clouds and little dolphins gracing the side.

"Is that what I think it is?"

"It's a floatie."

"These are for kids."

"So I'm a kid at heart."

"We're supposed to float on these little things?"

"They work great, all you have to do is get your feet just a little bit off the bottom. You sit on it, or lay on it and away you go. Some of the most fun we ever had as kids was to hike into these valleys, and float out. I always carry one for the backpack and one for me."

He handed it to her.

"You can have this one."

She looked at the stream, then back at the floatie. Her face brightened up. Things were looking better all the time.

"How long do you think it will take to get to the river?"

"Well, we're really only about a mile as the crow flies, but this stream meanders and loops all over the place before it gets there. All in all I think it's about a six mile run. It'll probably take us all day."

He picked up a stick and began to draw in the dirt.

"Okay, so here we are. The stream winds around and round, and down this valley like so, and comes out onto the river over here. There's a couple of little waterfalls right about here, and here, that we'll need to scramble down and around, but for the most part we'll just be floating and enjoying the scenery. As we get farther down the stream we'll come to some old irrigation ditches somewhere around here, that we can hop in for a faster ride down."

"So where is the so called secret waterfall, where this whole fiasco started?"

He made a mark in the dirt.

"Hale nu Kahili. Way over here."

21.

Kane, and the black suited SWAT team commander were studying the topographical map.

"We have the fire department's rescue chopper combing the surrounding area. Two teams are searching on the ground here and here."

He pointed to the map.

"We've sealed off the waterfall area," said the SWAT commander. "I don't want anyone tramping all over that zone. This is a crime scene now. What do you know about Grant?"

"Grant? He's just a big dumb kid. A big dumb rich kid."

"Well, he's a big dumb rich kid in a bunch of trouble. He's the last person to see Ashley."

"We always said he's about as sharp as a bowling ball."

"This morning the Governor ordered the National Guard unit on the island to mobilize and join in the search. That'll give us forty five boots on the ground. That's some thick jungle up there."

"One problem we're going to have is the weather. Clouds are building on the interior.

An outer band of the hurricane is about to hit us. Weather service says it's about two hours away, we should get a burst of rain wind and maybe some lightning for about half an hour. After that it'll clear up for a while, then the outer edges of the storm will hit around sunset, and the eye of the hurricane at midnight. We'll get the Navy rescue chopper from Hickam over here on the double. It has infrared ability, so we can see through any cloud cover."

Kane pointed to the kayak nearby.

"That's Tom O'Malley's kayak. Tied up to the same tree, hasn't moved all night."

"So now we have two missing people."

"Well, I wouldn't categorize Tom as missing. He goes camping for days at a time out there. Naw, he's not missing."

"Just goes camping huh? Is he a hunter, or a hippie, or a pot grower?"

"Tom? Naw, he's none of those things. He's got short hair and a job. He's just kind of what you might call a free spirit who likes being outdoors. I'd say he's more in his element up there, than down here."

22.

The line of cars at the gas station stretched out of the parking lot, spilling out onto the road, stretching for an additional hundred yards. Over a hundred cars all scrambling to get gas before the storm hit.

Kanui had waited in line in the old truck for nearly half an hour, and it had run out of gas two car lengths from the pump. Good timing.

Tom was still up in the mountains, he left the truck with the kayaks down by the river, and Kanui had to go retrieve it and stow away the boats, lash them in a big bundle with two hundred feet of rope to the coconut trees in Tom's back yard. Last thing they could afford to lose was the boats. He'd take the truck back down to the river, leave it in as safe a spot as he could find, as far away from the river as possible, but still close enough for Tom to locate it and get out of there. If he made it out before the storm hit. If not all bets were off.

He put the truck in neutral and got ready to push it the rest of the way to the pump. Lucky the surface was flat here, twenty minutes ago he on angle upslope and would have pulled a groin muscle getting it the rest of the way.

At noon the sirens went off. Tsunami warning sirens were scattered all around the island. They were tested at noon on the first day of the month, one long blast exactly forty five seconds. Except this wasn't the first of the month. It was the twentieth of July and a hurricane was making its final approach to the island.

You could see the worried look on just about everyone's face. The siren was un-nerving. It was a warning, and designed to rattle you, make you uncomfortable, and pay attention.

Danger was approaching.

He wasn't really worried about Tom. He could handle himself. He was really worried about Ashley. Everyone was. Sure she looked tough on the big screen, flying through the air like a female Tarzan, rescuing people from sinking boats, burning buildings, avalanches, exploding volcanoes. He'd even seen her in person waterskiing on the river and doing very well. But the back country was a whole different story. That was the real deal. Especially a back country with a hurricane on the way.

He'd been through two of them in his life. One when he was a baby. He didn't remember a single moment, and the other when he was a teenager where every second was imprinted on his memory banks. It was exciting at first, then semi-terrifying. Gusts of wind that sounded like a jumbo jet was about to land on your head, roofs lifting, lifting again, then flying like thousand square foot Frisbees through the air, crashing into parking lots full of cars, flattening everything. Avalanches of roof tiles billowing down the street as though a giant with a weed blower was hard at work.

Afterwards, the lush jungled mountainsides were completely barren as though a bomb had gone off. They saw contours in the valleys above them that had been hidden from sight for as long as anyone could remember. Giant trees snapped in half like brittle bones lining the ridges. Every leaf from every tree was stripped and there was a smell in the air, lingering, as though every single green thing on the island went through a shredding machine and was piled in a giant heap, decomposing in the tropical humidity.

The line in front started to move and Kanui leaned against the doorframe, pushing the truck forward. A car pulled in next to him and the window rolled down.

"Need some help?"

"Naw I got it," said Kanui, then recognized the voice. It was Carl from the convenience store. "Hey what's the latest Carl? I don't have a radio in this old jalopy."

"They said it might be edging away, might not be a direct hit after all. Just brush us with a lot of rain."

"Yeah right," said Kanui with a scowl. "That's what they said last time remember? Don't worry, it's gonna miss us, the track takes it away from us. And then KAPOW! Two hundred mile an hour winds right on top your noggin. Houses flying like the Wizard of Oz."

"Where's Tom?"

"Up in the valley."

"He's coming back down right?"

"I don't know, I haven't seen him in two days. He went up there to have a look around like he always says, but he never came back. He really went up there to see if he could help find Ashley Pepper. Any word on that?"

Carl shook his head.

"Yeah that's a big fat bummer, they're calling off the search till the storm passes, they can't have aircraft in the sky, or personnel on the ground. They're bringing everybody back."

23.

Tom sat on one of the inner tubes with the backpack on his lap, while Ashley followed close behind. They both have bamboo poles that they're using to push off the rocks on the edge of the stream as they pass. Here, the stream is gentle and clear.

Ashley uses her pole to spin around, holding her head back and watching the trade wind clouds in the blue sky.

"This is so fun."

"I told you."

"You know," she said. " You could make this an adventure ride. I'll bet plenty of people would pay for this."

"I have a tough enough time booking rides on the kayaks I have. I can't imagine trying to convince people that riding down the stream on an inner tube is fun. Not only that but the logistics involved getting them to hike all the way up here, then convincing them that sliding down a mud hill, flying into a stream and over a waterfall is a great idea."

She splashed him.

"Wise guy."

"So what's it like being a big movie star?"

She shrugged her shoulders.

"How would I know. I'm not that big of a star."

He frowned and splashed her back.

"Well I guess I am, but sometimes it doesn't seem real. It all happened pretty quick. And I'm not really used to the fast pace. It has its moments I guess. The limos, private jets, luxury suites. The grand dinners. That's all nice sometimes. But being a movie star means a lot of working inside. Make up, sound stages, interviews, rehearsals. They build a lot of stages to look like you're outside. Computer generated imagery. When they told me I needed to come here for a couple of extra shots, I couldn't get on the plane fast enough. I'm an outdoors kind of girl. I mean, look at this place."

Sunlight streamed through the trees, sparkling on the water.

"It doesn't get any better than this."

"I know," said Tom.

"So what about you, what's your story?"

"Me? Not much really. Just an average guy I guess. I was born on Oahu and we moved here when I was a year old, and I never left. Well, I mean for vacations and things like that. My dad was a fish and game warden for the state, sometimes he'd take me around with him, and I sort of got used to being outdoors. It fits me."

They heard the sound of a waterfall up ahead, and sure enough there was another infinity edge to the river.

"We'd better get out right over here," said

Tom, pointing to the side of the stream.

Soggy wet they stood at the top of a large waterfall looking over the edge. On either side of the cascading water sheer jungle covered cliffs dropped off to the valley floor fifty feet below them.

She looked over at Tom.

"Couple of little waterfalls on the way huh?"

"Yeah, I didn't remember it being this big. Or steep."

She looked back over the edge.

"I'm estimating a five story building Tom."

"At least. I remember climbing down the left side. There's a row of crevice's that zig zag down. Let's deflate the inner tubes and pack 'em in the backpack. I'll carry it."

Twenty minutes later they were ready. Tom crouched at the edge looking down ready to step into the first set of crevices.

"Piece of cake. Plenty of foliage to hang onto. You just have to grab onto the right one okay? Look for the guava branches, they're the strongest. I'll go first, you follow right behind me."

"This is scary. I don't know if we should do this."

"Don't worry, I've done this plenty of times. It's steeper than it looks. Trust me, I'm a professional.

He cracked a crooked smile.

She frowned.

"Let's go," he said as he crawled over the edge, testing the stability of his footing, trying not to put any weight on his injured ankle. He looked up at Ashley who had a panicked look on her face.

"C'mon now, I'm right here with you. Remember how you said you're an outdoors girl? Well it doesn't get much more outdoors than this."

"Grrr. Okay, just go slow." She crawled over the edge behind Tom, cringing inside, shaking on the outside.

Tom held onto a branch, while looking below for the next foothold. Ashley stepped on his hand, right on the edge of his knuckles. He tried to catch his breath, a sound wanted to leave his voice box but he didn't want to startle her, then it wheezes out;

"Gaaahhh…"

She looked down. The squishy foothold is attached to an arm.

"Sorry!" she whispers, holding on tight and yet her body unwilling to pull up the foot.

He waited until she lifted it a half inch.

"Just let me slide my hand out and you can put your foot there, okay?"

She nodded. He climbed down a notch and she put her foot where his hand just was. It seemed steady, she breathed a sigh of relief, then her foot began to slip, she scrambled to hold on, sliding downwards against the wall of the jungle.

"Help, help," the words are stuck in her throat, afraid to look down, cheek solid against the cool wall of the cliff.

Her foot found a secure spot, and she breathed another sigh of relief and looked down to see her foot is now wedged against Tom's contorted face.

"Do you mind?" he manages.

She slid her foot off his face, pointing the toe of her shoe into a crevice in the rock above his head, embarrassed.

"Sorry, I think I'm getting the hang of it."

"Follow right behind me, not on me, okay?"

"I'll try."

Tom was looking down. The cliff face has gotten steeper and there is less vegetation. Now what, he thought to himself.

"Alright," he said, making up his mind. "We're going to have to move just a little to the right. Just stick with me."

He crawled like a crab to the right, hanging onto a guava branch, continuing the descent. She followed behind trying not to look too far down.

They got into an unhurried pace, lowering themselves down the cliff face bit by bit. Time blurred as the only thing that mattered was the next foothold, the next handhold, slowly maneuvering downwards, steady and slow.

Sweat streamed down Ashley's face. A mosquito landed on her nose. She looked cross-eyed at it, tried to whoosh it off with some quick breathes. It won't budge. She carefully lifted the index finger of her right hand off the branch she's holding onto, put her face close and flicked at the bug. It still won't move. Now she can see it's little legs moving, settling into her skin, it's face pointing down, the needle coming out. She moved her face closer to her finger, crushing it, or so she thought, it was hard to tell if it was crushed or just moved somewhere else. She smiled with a semi-sense of triumph, then realized that her hand was slipping, the weight of her body too heavy for the half grip. She tried to re-grip but it was too late, she slipped farther down face of the cliff and landed on the valley floor after falling about two feet. She was at the bottom after all.

Tom was standing next to her smiling.

"Well that was a lot of fun," he said.

She gave him a friendly shove.

"Yeah, a lot of fun. I thought I was falling, why didn't you tell me we were at the bottom?"

"Sorry, I thought you knew."

"Well I didn't. Dang mosquito."

Tom took off the backpack, sat down on a rock and patted on another rock next to him.

"Have a seat and let's get these inner tubes filled up again."

He rubbed his hurt leg and stretched it.

"My leg's feeling a lot better now. Climbing down that cliff somehow loosened it up."

She sat down next to him.

"I was so scared I forgot about the pain in my ankle. Maybe we could have hiked out after all."

"Well it's too late now."

"I'm so hungry," she said with a hopeful look in her eyes. "Any more granola bars in that backpack?"

He shook his head.

"All tapped out. But we should definitely eat

something."

"All I see is jungle and green guavas."

"Ah, well that's where you're wrong. This place is full of food if you just know where to look. One though thing is for certain. We need to eat something. We need fuel for our bodies. We're still pretty far away and have one more little waterfall to climb down."

He opened up the backpack, took out the pot and a utility knife.

"C'mon, let's go find something to eat."

She followed him to the edge of the stream. In a shallow little eddy behind a pile of rocks a muddy area has formed, a backwater of sorts. In the mud is a small patch of green plants that look like elephant ears. He reached down cupping his hands into the mud and pulled two of the biggest ones by the roots, which look like potatoes. Each plant has seven elephant ear leaves of varying sizes, the largest the size of a basketball.

With the knife he slices off the leaves leaving a stub of stems growing out of the potato and lays them carefully on the side. Then he slices off the very tops of the potatoes and plants them back into the mud.

Then he began peeling the skin off the potato as he described it.

"This is taro, what they make poi out of. The scientific name is *colocasia esculenta*. You cut the top off, replant it and it grows again. Sort of a miracle plant. Very nutritious. This was one of the most important plants that the Hawaiians brought with them when they migrated here to the islands."

He washed the peeled taro in the stream, then cut it into slices into the pot, then rolled the leaves into balls, stuffing them on top of the taro.

He scanned the banks of the stream, and seeing something else, motioned for Ashley to follow. In a little clearing he cleared away a patch of purple flowers, and dug up some more long potato looking things.

"More taro?" she asked.

"Nope, these really are potatoes. Sweet potatoes."

"But how did..."

He motions for her to follow him again, this time to a patch of yellow flowers. He digs up the gnarled root, showing them to her.

"I give up," she says.

"It's a type of ginger. The Hawaiians call this Pua Olena, it's a type of turmeric. It'll give our dish some pop."

He went back to the stream, peeled the skin off the ginger, sliced them into the pot, then did the same with the sweet potatoes, but he held some on the side, placing them on a nearby rock, then filled the pot with water.

"Let's get this boiling."

He lit the sterno, placed four equal sized rocks around it, setting the pot on top, and covered it with a lid.

"It has to cook for an hour and a half."

"Why so long?"

"You see the Taro has these little calcium oxalate crystals that itch the inside of your throat if you eat it raw or undercooked. It's a toxin and can make your life miserable. Very important to thoroughly cook it. But that's okay, because we need another ingredient, and this one will take some time to catch."

Her face soured.

"We're not going to catch a pig are we?"

His face lit up.

"We could if you wanted. But, no it would take too long. This is much easier."

He scanned the stream bank, and saw the type of plant he was looking for. A type of fern with long slender leaves, shiny and strong.

He sliced three leaves, laid them on the ground and weaved them into a little basket. He took a long stem from one of the leaves and fashioned a little handle to go on top.

"Cute yeah?" he asked.

"Just adorable."

"You try."

He placed three leaves in front of her while he fashioned another basket.

She struggled at first, suspiciously watching him as he made the second basket. She fumbled, so he undid the basket, then re-assembled it. Now she had the method, tied the handle on top, beaming with success.

"I have no idea what I've just made, but here it is."

They each made two more, and now had five cute little leaf baskets with handles.

"Okay follow me."

"This is so mysterious." She whispered.

They went back to the rocks with the

steaming pot of food and the remnant pieces of sweet potato. He put a slice of potato into each container, then slid a small rock on top to hold it down.

Crouching like a hunter in the middle of the stream, he sank the baskets into a calm backwater eddy, then walked back to sit next to her.

"What are you trying to catch? Fish?"

"Fresh water shrimp."

"Get out."

"I kid you not. You see there's shrimp all over these streams, they're called Opae, they like clean fast moving water, the faster the better, they cling to the sides of the rocks with little pincers and grab bits of food as it travels down the stream. They're great climbers, and even climb up waterfalls. And one of the best things about them is they're attracted to sweet potatoes. They're pretty easy to catch, not many people know about it. They climb in through the little slits on the sides of these baskets, and while they're nibbling away at the potatoes, we'll haul 'em in."

"I'll believe it when I see it."

"There's snails too on the rocks if you're into that, Hihiwai and Pipiwai. Indigenous. Easy to get, just pry 'em off the rocks. They're about the size of your thumb. I don't really like them though. There's also five different types of fresh water Gobi fish that are called O'opu. Four are endemic and only found here, and another one is indigenous and are found all around Polynesia. The Hawaiians treasured them, white flaky meat. They're voracious predators, they'll eat any fish smaller than them. It's impossible to keep them in an aquarium with other fish because they'll eat anything smaller than them. We could catch the O'opu with the Hihiwai snail if we had a hook. But I didn't bring one with me."

His voice was soothing. Even though she didn't understand any of the Hawaiian words filtering out of his mouth, it was like hypnosis.

She laid down on a flat rock while listening to him and went straight to sleep.

A little more than an hour later he nudged her awake.

"C'mon, let's get our prawns."

She rubbed her eyes.

"I thought I was dreaming," she mumbled. Then realized that she was now awake, watching him wade back into the water and retrieve the baskets, and brought them back to set them next to her.

"Yee of little faith," he said.

Each one was teeming with half a dozen shrimp the size of a hot dog. He took them out and popped them right into the pot and closed it up again.

Twenty minutes later it was ready. He used the top of the pot for a plate and made her a dish, giving her the one fork and using his hands for the remainder in the pot. She was hesitant at first and then her eyes rolled back.

"This is..." she began to say.

"Fresh ginger prawns with sweet potatoes and taro."

"...incredible," finishing her sentence before taking another bite, savoring it with eyes closed. "There's this restaurant in Saint Tropez, on the French Riviera. Very famous. Very expensive. The chef there is extremely stuffy and full of himself, in my humble opinion. He also makes a ginger prawn dish."

"How's this compare?"

"Oh, ha..." she laughed at the thought. "He would blow a gasket. I mean he would literally pop his lid if he tasted this. Oh wow. I could just live here. Just set up a little tent right here and just live."

She breathed deep while sighing. Then her face lit up. Flush with the surge of amino acids from the food entering her system and the excellence of a thought.

"I know!" she shouted. "We should just camp here, set up the tent and camp. Forget about going down the stream. Just live a real life, right here."

"Sorry, no can do."

"Why not. You do it. All the time you said. Why can't I? I have just as much of a right as you do."

"What about all the adoring fans, the luxury, the stardom."

"Oh Tom, it's all fake. Most of it anyways. The magic of movies. Tinsel town. It can churn out some of the most miserable souls in the world. They start to believe they're better than anyone else, the rules for normal people don't apply to them. And then the hordes of people struggling to make it into the business. It turns into a struggle to survive. It's a dog eat dog world, and you're only as good as your last outing. Sometimes I'm afraid of it."

"I don't know Ashley. From I've seen so far, you seem pretty grounded. I mean look at you, sitting in the mud, eating roots and prawns from the river you've been swimming in. Doesn't get much more grounded than that."

She started to smile, and then bit her lower lip.

"That's another thing. Kind of ashamed of it now."

"What's that?"

"My name's not even Ashley Pepper. They made it up for me. Said it gave me more 'pizazz'. My dad was kind of upset when I changed it. I'm living a lie, living life as a stage name."

"Not Ashley Pepper?"

"Nope."

"Well what?"

"You'll laugh."

"I will not laugh."

"Penelope Lane."

Tom stifled a chuckle, holding his breath with all his might, clenching his fist against his lips then got hold of himself, then tried to be casual.

"Penelope. That's pretty old school. Wow. Like the roaring twenties old school."

"Lane. And my last name is Lane."

"Okay, so Penelope Lane. What's the big deal."

She tilted her head to the side.

"My nickname growing up was Penny."

He shrugged his shoulders.

"Penelope, Penny. Yeah, that makes sense. Penelope Lane. Penny Lane." Then he said it again, much slower, accentuating each syllable. "Penny Lane."

His face scrunched in thought. Why did those two words sound so familiar. He slapped his thigh as the answer came to him.

"Oh yeah, like the song. Penny Lane. The Beatles."

"That's me, or at least the real me. My parents struggled for days to come up with the perfect name for me when I was born. I didn't have a name for two days. And I then I change it for a job."

Her eyes narrowed and her mouth scrunched as she fretted over what she just told him.

Tom nodded. She was worried about her parents.

"Okay look, check it out. You see this valley we're in? It wasn't too long ago that it was chock full of Hawaiians. Maybe only a hundred years ago, give or take a few years. Families. Kids, old folks, teenagers. Living right here. That's where this taro, and ginger, and sweet potato come from. It grows wild now. But they're the ones that brought it here, and it still lives on. And for us to be here, and have a meal from this land when we're hungry, it's kind of like we're carrying on that legacy that they left. We're honoring it with good thoughts and good deeds. I don't know, I get caught up in it all when I'm in the valleys. You know, I think everyone's life is kind of like this valley. Your ancestors left you food for when you're hungry, spiritually, within you. You just have to know where to find it. It's there, in all of us."

She was stunned. Speechless, staring at him with an awestruck face.

"Whoa," he laughed, suddenly embarrassed. "Where did that come from."

She looked at him knowingly, with respect.

"Thomas O'Malley, you are a philosopher."

His face turned red and he waved at the air, trying to change the subject.

"Aw, it's just the setting."

He was silent for a moment, listening to the stream before continuing.

"But it's true. That's really how I feel, and I don't think I've ever told anyone. Till now. You know there's probably a lot of people really worried about you, and going out of their way to find you. C'mon Ashley Pepper, let's get you out of here."

Her eyes steadied on him.

"You can call me Penny."

His eyes did not waver.

"Alright then Penny Lane, let's get you out of this valley."

24.

They gently floated down the stream again. Not saying a word, for some reason it felt like no words needed to be said for a time.

Comfortable in each other's presence. Birds singing in the trees. Water gently flowing, carrying them with it.

White fluffy trade wind clouds from the morning had given way to towering strato-cumulus, the tops of the white fortresses billowing thousands of feet above the island, while the bottoms draped across the craggy peaks.

It started to sprinkle.

"Passing shower," said Tom hopefully while studying the shapes of the clouds.

He seemed to recall a tropical storm or a minor depression, or a front approaching the islands, but with all the action around the river the past couple of days, he'd forgotten all about it. These looked like pre-frontal convergence clouds, gelling up around the island, the tall jungled shrouded peaks gathering up the turbulence, slowing their progress, building their strength.

He tried to estimate their height. Fifteen,

twenty thousand feet maybe, and rising.

"What time do you think it is?" she asked.

He checked the location of the sun through the thickening clouds, shading the small orb with the edge of his hand.

"Probably a little after noon."

"Sure is getting dark."

Off in the distance they heard the sound of rolling thunder echoing off the mountain, and down through the valleys.

"Thunder," she said.

"Yeah, you don't hear that too often."

One of the problems with being on a stream in a valley that was surrounded by thousands of acres of other small nooks, niches, cracks in the hillsides, meandering creeks and tunnels that sloped down, small insignificant veins carrying their own tributaries of water, barely trickles of moisture in ordinary times, was that when a torrential downpour covered those thousands of acres with as little as an inch of rain, it translated to hundreds of thousands of gallons of water, all headed for the main tributary.

Tom knew this as much as anyone.

"Maybe we should try to hurry a little," he said in a calm voice, trying not to alarm her.

They pushed quicker now with their little bamboo sticks increasing their pace. Dark swirls of misty clouds brushed against the jungled walls and descended down into the valley nearly to the level of the stream.

The rain began to come down harder, drops the size of small marbles. More thunder, this time louder, rolling and bouncing off the valley walls around them.

She yelled out over the sound of the stream and the downpour.

"Is this safe?"

"I don't know!" he yelled back.

The rain was now coming down in sheets obscuring the valley. The stream began to swell, moving faster.

Now they were going so fast, the bamboo in their hands were being used to slow down to avoid the rocks.

A flash of lightning cracked the sky in half right above them, the BOOM of thunder not a split second behind.

"Let's get out!" Tom yelled.

He pointed to an eddy up ahead.

"Up there!"

He maneuvered towards the calm water. She struggled to get out of the middle of the stream, but it has her in its clutches. She passed right by Tom just as he's easing into the eddy.

"I can't slow down!" she shouted.

She spun out of control in the rapids. He braked on the bottom with his feet, lunging towards her with his bamboo pole. She reached out to grab it.

"Hang on!" he shouted.

Her momentum twisted her away from the pole, in the process twisting it against her thumb and out of her hand. She sped off down the stream. He pushed back into the stream to follow.

Now they're completely in the clutches of the rapids, Penny in the lead with Tom twenty feet behind.

A bright flash, another crack of thunder, the bolt of lightning split a tree next to the stream up ahead, the top half of it falling into the water in front of her.

She screamed and crashed into it. Her inner tube popped on a branch, and she held onto the limb as the water flowed around and over her. The tree is smoldering, the water wrenching, her grip slipping.

Tom ditched the backpack and bamboo pole into the swollen stream as he neared the downed tree. He slid into the water holding onto the inner tube by hooking his left arm into it. He slammed into the tree, grabbing onto a branch as the current tried to wrestle him away from Penny. He pulled himself towards her while holding out the inner tube.

"Grab it!" he shouted.

The water is raging over her, she's held in check by the log. She lets go with one hand, grabbing onto the tube, it bends in half, but does not break as he pulls her towards him. She lets go of the tree with her other hand, clinging to the tube in a death grip with both hands.

He pulled her towards the edge of the stream. The current eased for a moment then he grabbed her under her arms and they struggled out of the clutches of the water.

The backpack was gone, floating down the rapids past the tree. All they're left with is one inner tube and each other.

Another flash of lightning and instantaneous crack of thunder.

"Let's get away from this water!" he shouted, pointing to the valley wall.

They trudged through mud as fast as their feet could manage, pushing through the slick wet vegetation, and steady rain. Up ahead they spotted an overhang of rock and headed for it.

It was a little cave in the side of the cliff, ten feet round with a flat floor, perfect for camping if it came down to it. Sheets of water were shedding off the cliff face.

"Quick now," Tom warned. "Let's get inside."

They plunged through the mini waterfall into the dry dark cave. It was more than tall enough to stand in. Graffiti littered the walls on the interior with plus signs in between names and initials. They weren't the first couple to visit this spot.

Penny was shivering, partly from the cold, mostly from fear. Tom put his arm gently around her, not sure how she would react to his overture. Tears were streaming from her eyes. She pulled her long hair to the side and settled into his shoulder.

"I thought I was a goner."

"Aw, you're okay. Just a little ride down the rapids."

She pulled away and looked up at him.

"A little ride down the rapids? What about the lightning, and the tree?"

His face was incredulous.

"That? Oh, I've seen worse. Why one time when me and my friends were just little kids, we were riding down these rapids in a *real* rain storm, not a little bitty one like this, and lightning knocked down TWO trees in front of us. Now that was radical." He shook his head and scrunched his lips. "One tree is nothing."

That cheered her up. She smiled, and wiped the tears from her eyes.

She studied him, close as they were. He smiled back at her and winked.

"Now," he thought would be about the best chance he'd ever have in his life to try to give a beautiful movie star a kiss..

His mind flashed back to the old folks home, sitting with Doc.

"Look," Doc said. "All I'm saying is, next time you see an opportunity, take it. I don't want you to get to be my age and regret that you didn't."

Then just as suddenly, his mind flashed back to a few short hours ago, last night in the tent, Ashley warning him.

"Just keep your hands to yourself buster."

Now he was concerned, conflicted on what to do. When in a situation like this, always err on the side of caution. He gently took his hand off from around her shoulder, gave a little whistle and looked out the mouth of the cave at the stream.

"Hey, looks like it's letting up," he said.

She scrunched her lips together and narrowed her eyes suspiciously.

"You know Tom, it never came up in casual conversation during our little outing here in the valley, while floating down the stream, and I never asked if you had a girlfriend, or a wife."

She accentuated the word wife before

continuing.

"And I see that you're not wearing a ring. But sometimes that doesn't mean much."

He tried to make a joke of it, wiggling ten fingers and thumbs in the air.

"Hey, no rings, no strings." Then thought better of it. Might as well level with her that he was a schmuck and a loser. "Aw heck, it's an old sad story. I used to have a girlfriend a while back. She dumped me. Haven't thought about getting another one." He smiled at her. "Too much trouble."

"Why'd she dump you, were you mean to her?"

His smile faded, as a low grumble sound filtered up from his voice box. She wasn't going to let it go.

"We just didn't fit very well together if you know what I mean. She liked total comfort, and I like to rough it up once in a while. I like getting outdoors, camping in the wilderness, she liked high rises, restaurants."

"Well, if this is one of your typical camping trips I can't blame her."

"Funny. So what about you? You're a big movie star, probably have lots of boyfriends. Lapping at your feet like little puppy dogs."

Why, he thought to himself, am I suddenly being cruel to her?

"I don't read the tabloids by the way," he said, shrugging his shoulders, even though he bought them the old folks home every single week. "So I wouldn't know."

She sighed. "Aw yes. The tabloids. They've

hooked me up with just about everyone in Hollywood. Everyone."

"Yikes."

"None of it's true. I had the same boyfriend since high school till a few months ago. It just didn't work out. I dumped him."

He frowned.

"Sounds familiar. Don't tell me, he liked to go camping, and you didn't."

"Something like that. I found out he had another girl camping out at his house while I was away at a film location."

"Ouch."

"Ouch is right. I came home early to surprise him and walked in on them. I don't have to give you all the vivid details. They seemed to be having a good time. Boy was he surprised. Never seen a person so surprised in my life in fact."

"Double ouch."

"In a way it was partly my fault."

Now it was his turn to look at her suspiciously, wondering what kind of debauchery might have happened on location.

"How so?" he asked hesitantly. Almost not even wanting to know.

"I signed a big contract with the studio. Three films, three years. One of the conditions was that I appear to be 'available'. They said it made me a bigger draw. He felt left out, went looking around and found someone else. I just wish he would have leveled with me, instead of just going along with it till he couldn't stand it anymore. I haven't even thought about being with anyone else since." She tilted her head and frowned. "Too much trouble."

No debauchery. Just a miserable contract.

"So how many more films do you owe them?"

She smiled.

"One more to go, and then I'm free."

They were silent for a moment watching each other, and then it happened as naturally as the rain falling from the sky. Each moving the same slow speed towards each other they molded together perfectly from head to toe.

Lips gently touching, hands caressing, her soft body and breasts pressing up into him, he pulled her closer, her back arching, she sighed.

Heat flowing between them slowly becoming unbearable. He reached down, unlatching the button on top of her shorts and slid them over her hips then lifted her high until she wrapped her legs around him. She reached down, unbuttoning his pants till they fell down around his ankles. Rock hard, deep soft, he lifted and lowered her over and over until she threw her head back, crying out as a bolt of lightning lit the cave, thunder exploding, echoing off the walls and down throughout the valley.

She lay her face against his shoulder as their heaving breaths slowed. They could feel each other's heartbeat thumping loudly against their chests.

The rain came down steady, unrelenting. She gently put one foot then the other down onto the ground, still leaning against him. Face planted firmly on his shoulder, not wanting to let go.

"Where did that come from," she whispered.

He had no idea, but cold reality was catching back up to him.

"I'm just a tour guide you know," he said as he kept his arms wrapped around her, not wanting to let her to get away, not yet.

There were all kinds of words she could tell him, but only one thing was as true as the falling rain.

"You saved me," she whispered.

In more ways than one.

She finally lifted her face away from his shoulder, for the first time in a very long time feeling safe in someone's arms. He wasn't going to let her go, but the question needed to be asked.

"So what now?"

He nodded. Reality.

"We're still in a bit of trouble. We need to get out of this valley. Then we can figure it out. My job, as your personal tour guide is to get you safe and sound back to civilization."

Reluctantly buttoning their clothes, on the verge of embarrassment at the ferocity of their sudden animal like action, she blushed, and his face slackened, the blood leaving him ashen in self- doubt.

She smiled then reached up and kissed him gently, leaving one hand on his chest while whispering in his ear.

"Can we come back again someday?"

His eyes lit up with her lips brushing against

his earlobe.

The green light.

Dumb as a rock, as though he'd stumbled through a magic gate into nirvana, the only word he could muster was;

"Yup."

The rain doubled in volume, taking on a different crescendo.

"Wow," she said. "it's really coming down hard now."

He tilted his head, angling his right ear towards the opening of the cave. The sound had changed. Giant buckets of water walloping out of the sky.

"That's not the rain, that's a helicopter."

The steady thump of a hovering aircraft rumbled overhead. They scrambled out of the cave looking up into the clouds and rain which were too thick and obscured any view of the machine.

"That's no ordinary helicopter," he said. "I hear the tour helicopters all day long heading over the mountains. They're little gnats compared to that one. That's a big copter, probably military. Looking for you."

The sound of it passed by heading downstream, down the valley and away. The thumping blades slowly faded out, leaving them standing in the rain, in the silence.

"We'd better keep moving," he said. "We haven't heard any thunder for a while now. It usually moves in along the edge of the front. These things move pretty quick in the islands. I wouldn't be surprised if the sun came out in about an hour from now. At any rate we'd better keep moving. We've got no tent, no food, no way to make food, and we don't want to be stuck in this valley when it gets dark."

She followed his lead reluctantly leaving the safety of the cave. She looked longingly back at the entrance, trying to memorize its location in the middle of the jungle, in the hope of coming back this way again, and if not, if for some reason she never made it back again, if they never made it back, she could hold on to the memory of the brief pure moment, at very least for a foothold, a strong guava branch to hold onto as she climbed down the cliff of life.

They moved through the jungle next to the stream. The going was slow. The rocks covered in wet moss, slippery, the ferns pulling at them.

"This will take forever," he lamented.

"I don't suppose we want to get back in the stream," she asked.

They stopped and studied it. The water was still swelling up to the banks. Maybe they could float at the edge of the stream, but the rapids at the center were full and travelling fast, forming waves at it swept over the rocky bottom, the sound was intense. They'd be swept right into it again.

He shook his head.

"Not yet it's still moving too fast, not only that, but look over there."

There was a clearing up ahead. The valley opened up wider past the clearing, they were leaving the narrowest part of the valley up to this point in time. The stream ended suddenly, disappearing over an edge. An infinity edge. There was a roaring sound climbing up and over that edge towards them, a huge ball of mist rising in the air.

"Waterfall?" she whispered.

"That's the second one. Do you believe in divine intervention?"

Tom looked back up the stream, and she followed his eyes. Far back up the valley just past the location of the cave was a giant pile of branches covering a car sized trunk of wood laying over the rapids.

"The tree," she said.

"Cut down by a bolt of lightning."

"I couldn't get out of the water, the current was too strong, dragging me towards..."

They were both silent as the definitive reality sunk in.

"Dragging you towards the waterfall," he finished.

"Alright," he said finally. He had to keep her fighting spirit up. No time to get weepy about what might have happened. It was time to get strong. "That's in the past, we need to move forward. Let's go. Okay?"

He grabbed her hand and squeezed it gently.

"Okay," she said, and tried to smile.

They made their way to the edge of the waterfall and kept a safe distance while looking over the precipice.

"This one's bigger," she said.

"Yeah." He whistled.

The other waterfall was less than half the size of this monster. Fifty feet across, over a hundred feet high, the water volume so fierce that it shot out from the edge horizontally in a thunderous cascade, billowing mist filling the valley from top to bottom in front of them.

He scanned the valley walls, carefully, taking his time, visualizing the descent, it was like a giant curved bowel, steepest right at the waterfall, a vertical drop where they were standing. They had to get farther over away from the falls.

"There," he pointed. "Down the left side. This is where we go down. I can see it. We'll have to shimmy over a little bit of a steep area and then angle down."

He looked back at her.

Fear was in her eyes. Hesitating before answering.

"If you say so."

He smiled to give her confidence, and winked.

"Piece of cake. Same plan. I go first to test the path, and you follow."

The first part was easy. A subtle incline, thick jungle, solid rocks. Seemingly a path heading down that was well used by hunters, goats, or both. Crawling down the valley wall like crabs on all fours. The ferns and vines wet with the steady rain.

Penny struggled. Her foot slipped and she caught herself, gripping tight on a branch, pressing her face against the wall, taking a deep breath.

"Piece of cake," she whispered to herself.

Tom could see that she stopped and called

out to her.

"How're you doing?"

"Oh just peachy."

She looked down at his face, trying not to look past him, but there in the distance was the rock strewn bottom still very far away. She tried to smile, but just sighed, taking a deep breath, looking for the next place to set her foot, right above where his hand was.

"Once you get to where I'm at it gets easier."

"Okay."

And then she slipped again, but can't catch herself. She grasped at branches and ferns as she slid down, too shocked to scream.

"Penny!" he yelled.

After sliding fifteen feet straight down her arm caught in the loop of a vine and she came to a stop. Her feet searched out and found two little nooks to scrabble into. She's shaking and can't breathe, pressing her face against the rock.

"I can't move, can't move," she whispered.

Tom is above her now and to the right on the valley wall.

"Hang on," he said steadily.

He crawled down and over towards her, and got to within an arm's length away. He dug his feet into a long rock crevice, grabbed onto a guava branch with his right hand and reached his left hand towards her.

"Grab my hand," he said with a steady, unhurried voice.

"I can't move," she whispered. Her cheek is flat against the rock, facing away from him.

"Just move your right hand over towards me."

"If I let go of this vine I'll fall."

"You're not going to fall. I can see your left arm wrapped in the vine. Just reach out with your right hand. I'll grab it."

She lifted her face lightly, rotating it towards him while keeping some skin always touching the rock, sliding her nose over it until she could see his face.

"Don't let me fall."

"Never."

She steadied her left arm looped in the vine, slowly releasing her right hand, sliding it across the rock wall till their fingertips touched. The vine creaked with the shift in weight. His hand wrapped tight around the center of her forearm while her hand did the same with his creating a serpentine arm lock.

The vine snapped.

She fell straight down, then swung towards him, grabbing onto his legs with her right hand, her feet finding a ledge right below.

They were motionless for a moment, not wanting to move. The rock crevice where his feet were lodged began to stress and crack. Small pebbles crumbled and fell away on top of her head. He looked over at the guava branch that he's holding onto, and it started to bend from the weight.

"C'mon guava," he whispers. " Don't let us down."

He gritted his teeth reached down and pulled her up till she was standing on the rock ledge with him, both of them holding onto the guava branch that stretched horizontally above them.

"Now you stay right here," he said. "This branch is yours, I'm going to move to the right just about two feet. Then we'll do the arm bar again. If you look right over there," he motioned with his head to the side. "There's safety, and it's only four or five feet away."

"Well which is it," she asked, voice cracking.

"What?"

"Is it four or five feet. I need to know."

He looked over and mentally measured it. She needed an exact amount.

"It's four feet. We'll go two feet at a time. Okay?"

She nodded.

He could tell that she needed a moment to catch her breath and steady herself, but there was no time to waste. Arms got tired, feet got tired, suddenly and without warning you could go into a sort of physical shock, lose all sense of balance and strength. He moved to the right. Repositioned his feet. Held out his left hand, wrapping around her right hand.

"Now step to the right, put your foot right next to mine. Slide it next to mine, that's it."

Coaching her, she wedged her right foot up against his.

"Bring your left hand over and grab the root above your head, and then slide your left foot up against your right."

When she got that accomplished and was wedged tight against the wall and secure, he slid his right foot over two feet, found the crevice with his toes, wedging them tight, slid his right hand over two feet and they went through the process again.

Now, below him was a gentle rise that led to the side of the cavernous bowl they were climbing down into. Eroded debris from the sharp edge of the cliff over the eons had piled up enough in this area to create a slope embedded with trees and ferns. Slightly less severe than a vertical cliff to begin with right below their feet, it curved gently ending down to the valley floor. They slid over, two feet at a time until they were safely on the slope. Now, even if they lost their footing or the ground gave way, myriads of trees and bushes would halt their progress.

Slowly winding down the hill, scraped and bruised, they set foot finally on the horizontal surface on the valley floor. Tom got there first and reached up to help her the last step.

She put her arms around him, hugging him tight for a long time, the fear of falling off the cliff, that she subdued in the darkest moments coming back to her now that she was safe, then as her breathing began to even out, listening to the beat of his heart, she calmed down, wiped a tear from each eye and stepped away.

They each found a flat rock to sit on, looking with wonder at the cliff that they in hindsight foolhardily climbed down. Somehow it didn't look as steep and treacherous from this angle as it had when they were halfway down it clinging to vines and branches. The rain had stopped and some blue sky began to peak through the swirling grey clouds.

"What'd I tell you," said Tom. "Look for the guava tree." Ever the pragmatist he continued, attempting to console her. "That wasn't so bad eh?"

She looked sideways at him, narrowed her bloodshot eyes, and shook her head. Why be a baby about it. It was in the past. She was getting the hang of Thomas O'Malley's rule number one of life. The good things you hold onto, but the bad things you let go, they're in the past where they belong and they can't hurt you anymore. She smiled and shrugged her shoulders. "Yeah, it wasn't so bad."

"Are you kidding me?" he chided her, then laughed heartily. "I've never been so scared in my life. I don't know what I was thinking. But I'll tell you one thing for sure, I will never climb down *that* waterfall again, not on this side anyways. Next time, if there ever is another time, I'm taking the other side."

She finally chuckled. "You're crazy."

"Check out the stream," he said pointing towards it. Seems a little less wild."

She looked cross-eyed at him. "Are you sure there aren't any more waterfalls downstream?"

"Positive. Look at the valley around us, see how it's evened out? We're just a few hundred feet above sea level, and this little valley opens right up ahead into the main big valley. We're almost home."

"We've only got one inner tube," she said.

"We can share it. You sit on it, and I'll hold

on from the side. If there's a problem up ahead, I'll be able to stop us and pull us out."

She shook her head. "You'll get pummeled by the rocks. The water is moving too fast. I say no."

After the fiasco of the waterfall nearly ending in tragedy, he relented.

"This is your adventure too. Let's keep walking."

The progress was slow, but seemed safer than plunging into the rapids again, with no guarantee that they could extricate themselves. The rocks bordering the stream were slippery so they ventured away from it, finding flat muddy ground to slop through.

They found a pig trail. following it until it disappeared into the jungle, suddenly becoming a hole in the vegetation three feet high burrowing into the bushes.

Up ahead they saw a structure, and headed straight for it. It was a broken down wooden gate next to the stream. The wood silver with age, rotten on the ends, mottled with black and green mold. It was protecting a concrete wall that was built adjacent to the stream. The concrete walls began perpendicular to the stream, then bent abruptly at a forty five degree angle away from the stream. It was diverting water into a four foot wide, four foot deep ditch covered with ferns and jungle growth, moss, lichens, small trees. It disappeared into the shadows in the distance.

A rusted metal sluice gate with a round steering wheel to lift the gate is permanently rusted half open, letting the water flow into the trench.

"Old irrigation ditch," said Tom. "It runs for about a mile, and comes out somewhere down near the river, or it may just peter out in a field somewhere. Either way it's a lot safer than riding down the rapids right now. These things are everywhere. They dug them all over these hills and flatlands about a hundred years ago, and they still work. They were used to irrigate the sugar cane fields. Super fun to ride down. Some tour companies even charge money to bring people up here."

He winked at her.

"But today, we get to ride for free."

She was unimpressed.

"Looks creepy."

"Yeah it is, and fun. C'mon this is the last leg of our little journey, we're almost out. Look how slow that water's moving."

He took the folded inner tube out of his pocket, and started blowing it up.

She eyed the ditch with suspicion.

"Are you sure it's safe?"

He smiled at her.

"Piece of cake."

"Oh brother."

He climbed over the sluice gate, down into the canal, steadying himself, then held up his hand to help her down.

"Alright, here we go, you just sit in the middle of the tube, and I'll hold onto the sides."

She stood with her hands on her hips, then sighed once and climbed down.

The water was muddy but moving slow and steady, hardly a ripple on the surface. Like a kiddie ride after what they've been though.

The going was easy, the greenish water flowing smooth and flat. The clouds were clearing, the sun shining bright, the sky turning a deep blue above them.

"Looks like the storm is gone," said Tom.

The jungle passed by, the sun filtering through the trees above and around them.

She reached out to let the ferns brush her hands as they travelled along in silence, looking with wonder at the wild tangle of green, the sound of the gentle water, birds singing in the distance.

"This is actually fun," she said.

"I told you it would be."

"I guess it wasn't such a bad trip down the stream."

He laughed.

"A couple of bumps in the road. Minor. Sometimes it's fun to get out and test your boundaries. Obstacles are put in your path, you find a way around them. You deal with situations as they arise. That's what makes a life. Keeps you on your toes. You did great up there."

She corrected him. "WE did great up there. Shooting the rapids, climbing down those cliffs. Making a gourmet meal in the middle of nowhere."

Silence again as the quiet sounds of the water flowing along the canal permeated the air. Neither of them wanted to talk about it but they were both thinking about the sudden brief moment in the cave, the rain and lightning.

She shivered, not from the cold water, then continued.

"Right now Mr. O'Malley I'm not looking forward to going home."

His face remained stoic. He answered casually.

"So don't go."

"It's not that easy. A lot of people are relying on me. I'm under contract for another movie, they're probably lining up the shooting schedule right now. I can't just walk away. Not yet. But I've learned a lot the past couple of days."

"Oh yeah?"

"Like you said. Sometimes it's fun to test your boundaries. Keeps you on your toes... And what the heck is that thing up there?"

The jungle closed in. Up ahead was a small dark tunnel. The ditch funneled straight into it, disappearing into a black hole.

Tom put on the brakes, digging his feet into the muddy bottom, bringing their progress to a halt.

They peered into the tube and could see daylight shining far at the end.

Ashley shook her head.

"I am not going in that thing."

"Are you kidding me," chided Tom. "This is the funnest part."

"Are you out of your mind? Can't we just go around it?"

"You see how thick this jungle is? To hike

around it would take around an hour, maybe more. We can zip through it in about three minutes."

"Zip through it," she deadpanned.

She peered down the length of it, grimacing.

"C'mon," he continued. "Don't be a baby. I've been down plenty of these. They're easy. You've seen one you've seen 'em all.

She hesitated like a trapped animal, ligaments taught, ready to flee. Then her shoulders slumped while her body went limp with resignation.

"Oh, all right. I guess after what I've been through today, this should be pretty tame."

"Now we're talking."

"So what do we do?"

"Just duck."

They headed into the tunnel, and everything went dark.

"Don't worry," he said. "Our eyes will adjust."

"Piece of cake," she whispered, closing her eyes to help the adjustment process quicken.

When she opened her eyes again, they were passing by openings in the sides of the tunnel where they could see green jungle shining through,

"What are those?"

"Access panels. In case the tunnel gets plugged they can send a worker with a shovel to unplug it."

"They look like escape hatches."

"We're about halfway through. Almost there."

They heard a sound above them, faint at first, as though someone was tapping on top of the tunnel with two hands, tapping like they were playing on a bongo drum. It got louder. Thumping now.

"What's that sound," she asked. "It's creeping me out."

If she could only see his face, she would see a frown as he shook his head in disgust.

"What is that sound?" she asked again, anxiously, as it began to echo throughout the tunnel.

"You don't want to know," he said as the thumping got louder till it seemed as though it was right on top of them, shaking dust from the top of the tunnel with the vibration.

"It's a helicopter," she said simply. "If we would have waited five minutes it would have seen us." But there was a tinge of fear in her voice. Now at the halfway point in the tunnel she began to feel claustrophobic, the walls were closing in on her and she began to have trouble breathing. Short quick breaths were not enough to sustain her and yet she could not take a complete breath. She had lost control.

"Get me out of here," she gasped lightly in between breaths.

He could sense the fear and pushed off the bottom behind to quicken their pace. The opening at the end began to get bigger and closer. Safety was in sight.

She smiled as the light from the end of the tunnel lit up her face.

Slowly, that smile faded right back into

sheer absolute fear.

Claustrophobia turned into Arachnophobia.

Up ahead the light was obscured, by some sort of faint cloud structure hanging down from the ceiling. Coming into focus was a tangle of spider webs all the way to the surface of the water.

"Uh oh," said Tom as he saw them.

They passed through the webs. Ashley screamed, her shrieks echoing through the tunnel as she pulled the sticky filaments from her hair into the water.

"Get off me!" she shouted, flailing her arms.

Since she was in the lead, all the webs have wrapped around her. Tom is frantically pulling at them from behind. One large spider is crawling across the back of her head. Tom saw it and grabbed at it.

"Spider on the back of your head," he said nonchalantly in explanation, grabbing it with his right hand, and flinging it into the water.

Another spider is crawling across the innertube and she swatted it off, then splashed water up into her face and hair.

"Are they all gone?" she asked breathlessly.

"I think we got 'em all. No need to worry about them, they're pretty harmless."

Up ahead they were quickly approaching the end of the tunnel.

"We're almost out," she sighed.

With the additional light, Tom saw another spider crawling across the top of her head.

"Uh Ashley."

"If you say piece of cake, I'll scream."

"There's another spider."

She felt it's little legs on top of her head, and screamed at the top of her lungs, both of them slapping at the top of her head, their hand smacking into each other.

They exited the tunnel going fast, too fast in fact to see that the water went right off the edge of sluice.

There was no way to stop. The bottom inside the cave is dark and so no moss grows, but here near the light at the end of the tunnel, the moss is thick on the bottom and slicker than oil. Tom tried to put on the brakes with his shoes, and grabbing on to the sides of the tunnel but it was too late. Ashley continued screaming as they plunged over the edge into a deep pool below. They flailed underwater, the tube hit a rock and popped.

After a small eternity of bubbles and currents pulling at them, they rose to the surface, then struggled to the edge. Tom threw the deflated tube onto the bank as they crawled out.

"So much for that."

Penny pulled the hair away from her face as Tom grinned at her.

"Well, look at the bright side," he said. "At least there's no more spiders."

"Grrrr, I hate spiders."

He stood up, surveying their surroundings. The pond that they landed in was the end of the road as far the stream was concerned. The edges flowed out onto a grass filled plain, little rivulets stretch off like veins downhill then disappeared into the tall grass which ranged from ten to fifteen feet high. This was the edge of once vibrant sugar cane field. You could still see black plastic drip lines broken in pieces scattered in the dirt.

He could see that she was still shaken up by the trip down the irrigation tube and the spiders.

"Let's catch our breath for a moment," he said. "I'll give you the local botany lecture. You see this tall grass? Well we're going to have to fight our way through it to get back to the river so you might as well know the story behind it."

He took a blade from the bottom of one of the clumps, holding it up to the light. The blade was close to ten feet tall, the width of his little finger, light green with a ridge running down the backside.

"It's fairly sharp on the edges, and there's little hairs all along the backside that are kind of like needles, so if you grasp onto it too tight with your bare hands, you'll regret it, like tiny little needles that will itch, and the only remedy is to wash it vigorously with water."

He gave it to her so she could feel it with her own hands.

"This is called guinea grass, it's one of the worst invasive species that we have in Hawaii. It takes over everything, it's tough, resilient, flood proof, drought proof, and is a major fire hazard. Some people call it Buffalo grass, including me on some occasions. It's so tough that when it gets this size it takes a herd of buffalo to get through it. The scientific name is

Megathyrsus maximus. Brought to Hawaii in eighteen forty seven by the cattle ranchers for supplemental feed. The native pili grass which is thin and small and not as nutritious, wasn't as prevalent or sufficient in quantity to feed all the cows."

"What happened," he continued. "Is that around seventeen ninety three, a captain of a trading ship was trying to make friends, and inroads so he could trade in peace here in Hawaii. Captain Vancouver was his name. He gave King Kamehameha six cows and a bull. The king created a four hundred acre pasture surrounded by a rock wall and placed a kapu on killing the cattle so that they could grow in numbers. By the mid-eighteen hundreds there were over twenty five thousand wild cattle roaming around the islands. That's about the time when all this buffalo grass was imported and took over."

"King Kamehameha III lifted the kapu during his reign and in the following years, ranches were established and Spanish vaqueros were brought in to help teach Hawaiians how to manage all these cattle."

"Over time, the ranches provided dried salted beef, also called pipikaula for sailors and hides for the New England tanneries, then production shifted to producing local beef for their communities, and finally adopting a grain finishing program for local beef production."

She was laying in the grass, listening to him, his voice soothing again. Putting her to sleep like listening to someone read statistics from the farmer's almanac on a hot summer afternoon. The monotony of the sounds like a sleeping pill. The words melted together, undecipherable.

He kept on talking, using his hands now and then to illustrate a point, chock full of useful information if you were a cattle farmer, or historian while she slept soundly.

He finally looked over at her, triumphant with his speech and knowledge of a subject so mis-understood, to see her eyes closed in peaceful slumber.

This was the second time today that she'd fallen asleep while he was talking to her.

"I must be the most boring guy in the world," he whispered.

He chuckled and sat down next to her. Might as well let her sleep for a few moments. They were almost out of here, the bad part was behind them. The grass was high where they were headed, behind them rose the mountain and the valley where they'd just come from. Somewhere on the other side of this wall of grass was the main river. Half a mile he estimated, give or take a hundred yards. Eight hundred, maybe nine hundred yards, eight football fields and they'd be free.

After about ten minutes, he gently pushed on her shoulder.

Nothing. Her eyes stayed closed. Breathing steady, no change.

This wahine, thought Tom, is one sound sleeper. Out here in the middle of nowhere and she just conks out.

He pushed on the shoulder again, then shook it lightly. Finally she stirred, eyes fluttered open.

"Wouldn't you agree?" he asked her.

"Huh? What?" She was confused, suddenly roused from a mini coma.

"So I'm the most boring guy in the world eh?"

She sat upright.

"Did I say something in my sleep? I felt like I was riding on a cloud. You were talking. Six cows and a bull."

He laughed. She blushed and smiled.

"You know Tom, there's a market for ultra-soothing voices that put people to sleep. You could make a fortune."

"I think it only works on you. Are you ready?"

She nodded her head and he helped her to her feet.

He picked up the flattened inner tube, folded it carefully then put it in his pocket. She was looking at him curiously with arms folded.

"Hey," he explained. "We don't want to litter."

He looked up in the sky setting towards the west over the mountain. The winds were hot and humid, coming from the south.

"I think it's about three o'clock. One more hour and we'll be out of here."

They pressed forward through the buffalo grass. It was so thick that you could lean against it, put your whole body weight against it and it would hold you up. The key was wedging your way through it. Finding a break in the bunches, weaving your way forward.

Just to the right and about half a mile away, appearing above the tassels of grass, they could see a distinctive outcropping of rock. Black and square jutting from the side of a small hill. Tom grinned and pointed at it.

"See that? The river goes right next to that rock hill. We're almost there."

They struggled over mounds of old logs and rocks for nearly half an hour. The air was thick, the winds cut off by the tall grass, sweat rolling down their brows, their breaths heavy.

Ashley was wearing out. She stopped, leaned over with her hand on her knees.

"I don't think I can go another step."

"Don't give up, we're almost there."

"So thirsty," she gasped. "I miss the stream. Even though we couldn't drink out of it. It was so cool and refreshing compared to this."

"Don't worry, a few more steps and you'll have a BIG stream to play in. Listen."

He held up his hand and they stood motionless. The faint sound of water filtered towards them.

"Water," she whispered.

"Lots of it."

The grass ended, and now they faced a twenty foot tall, twenty foot wide wall of tangled branches, with big round leaves and yellow flowers. They could see the water glistening through the wall of bark and leaves.

"Great," he whispered.

"Now what?"

"Hau bush."

"How in the heck are we going to get through that mess. Can't we just go around it?"

He thought hard while searching up and down the length as it disappeared in a morass, dense mix of hau and buffalo grass. There wasn't going to be any going around it.

"If memory serves me correct. This entire stretch of river upstream from the trail to the secret waterfall is covered in hau bush. We're just going to have to go straight through it. Remember when you were a kid in a jungle gym? Well this is kind of like that. Follow me."

The branches themselves were fairly uniform in width and circumference roughly the size of the end of a baseball bat and larger, curving and twisting, intertwining in a curious free form of creeping jungle. You could just about but not quite wrap your hands around the branches, but just get enough of your fingers around it for some grippage while bending your body through the tight spaces, feet slipping on the branches growing along the muddy ground. The going was slow but steady, with the river getting closer with each branch.

"Since you're not laying down, maybe I can give you one last native plant lesson without you falling asleep on me."

"Sure," she winced while squeezing like a contortionist through a tangle of branches and sizing up the next barricade.

"This is another canoe plant, brought by the Hawaiians on purpose."

"To torture people?"

"It's actually a hibiscus plant that grows all throughout Polynesia. It's scientific name is *Hibiscus tiliaceus*. It was so valuable that you had to have permission from the Chief to cut it. It's lightweight and buoyant, and the way it curves if you can find the right piece, makes it perfect for the outrigger canoe, the two booms that stretch out from the canoe, and the float itself."

He paused and looked back at her to make sure she wasn't going to sleep.

"I'm listening," she said while slipping between two branches.

"They use the wood for floats on fishnets, the bark for rope. It's good for making fires. You make a groove in the soft wood, then quickly rub a hard wood in the groove with a little pile of coconut fiber till it sparked. You can make spears, sandals, fences, shelters."

He squeezed through the last lattice and turned to help her through. They stood on a narrow mud bank next to the river at last.

It sparkled in the afternoon sun. At this point it was only about a hundred yards wide. Dark green water, moving slowly, the surface smooth and glassy, small whirlpools forming here and there.

"So beautiful," she said softly.

"I told you I'd get you here."

She smiled and patted him on the shoulder.

"Piece of cake."

His face though was firm. He pointed down the river, back to all business. A tour guide with a precious cargo, a valuable ward on the last leg of a treacherous journey. A small hurdle yet to cross, an innocent question that needed to be asked.

"We're not done yet. We're about two hundred yards from the drop zone for the waterfall hike. It's just around that bend in the river. The water's pretty deep here. Can you swim?"

The minute he said it, he regretted it.

"Can I swim?" she repeated. Her eyes narrowed, lower lip tensing. "Am I a child? Can I swim? Now you ask me. After travelling down five miles of streams, rapids, waterfalls, dark pipes full of spiders. Can I swim."

His diplomacy disappeared, it was a simple question, he needed a simple answer, he was hungry, thirsty, tired, injured, his voice raised a notch as though he was in fact speaking to a child.

"Well can you or not?"

She shook her head resigned in the absurdity of the situation, then managed a giggle.

"Yes, boss man, I can swim."

His magnanimous spirit returned and he wrapped his arms around her then said softly.

"That's all you had to say. Let's go."

He eased into the water, floating on his back.

"Aww, this is great."

He luxuriously laid out on top of the water. Ears immersed, eyes pointing straight up at the bright blue skies interspersed with fluffy white clouds. All was silent in his world.

She shook her fist at him, unseen, while still

playfully angered by his question of whether or not she could swim.

"I could beat you in any swimming race buster!" she shouted out.

He was shaken out of his watery slumber by the muffled sound of her voice, splashing his head clear of the water to look questioningly at her.

"What?"

"Oh nothing," she said sweetly while following his lead, easing into the water, then floating on her back, a sigh of relief sliding through her lips. "So tired," she whispered.

"Don't fall asleep on me," he said loudly.

He started a slow backstroke, while she followed.

"Let me know if I'm going too fast for you," he said, seriously. "We need to stick together. If you get tired and need a break, we can hold onto the hau branches hanging into the water, or find a little place where it's shallow, and we can stand and rest for a while."

She swam steadily, also doing the backstroke with a poised natural rhythm, then pulled in front of him, smiling at him as she passed.

"I still hold the record in the hundred yard backstroke at my high school."

He tried to pick up the pace, but it was too late, she got a body length ahead of him which turned into two then three before he gave up.

She looked back to see that he was floating and barely moving, trying to catch his breath, and she gave up too, the thrill of competition overtaken by bone tired fatigue.

She switched to a modified back-breastroke, legs like a leapfrog, and let him catch up.

Ten minutes later they rounded the bend in the river, then went down the little side alley and could see Toms kayak, just where he left it. It was the only boat there, still tied to the trees along the bank.

Too tired to smile, they swam the breast stroke the remaining few feet, then stood on the muddy bottom. Tom held out his hand, pulling her towards the bank.

"C'mon champ," he said. "We're almost home."

He helped her into the front seat of the kayak, then slipped into the back with one fluid move while pushing it away from the river bank. They were floating again.

"Sorry, I've just got this one paddle."

"That's okay," she smiled, leaning backwards in the front seat, hands intertwined behind her head, legs stretched up along the front.

"Last leg of the journey," he said. "Something you can tell your friends about someday, when you're lounging by the pool in Malibu, or on vacation in the French Riviera."

"But it wasn't a piece of cake," she said matter of factly.

"No?"

"Nope."

"Well what then?"

She smiled at the thought of it.

"It was just a walk in the park Thomas O'Malley. Just a stroll through a big giant wonderful park, and now that it's all over, I wouldn't mind doing it again."

He didn't answer her right away, smiling gently while dipping the paddle into the river, reminiscing about the best tour he'd ever been on. A tour he'd have to forget all about if he was ever going to have any kind of life in the future.

He had to be pragmatic about the events of the past twenty four hours. She would get on a plane and leave. And once she was back in the whirlwind of her life, she would also have to forget about it, in order to survive in that hectic world that she chose. His smile faded, but his paddling remained steady.

"Yep, that it was Penny Lane. That it was. Just a walk in the park."

25.

The red fire department helicopter set down in the landing zone hastily marked the day before as a yellow circle with an X in the middle. Three firefighters exited the chopper from the back seat, and headed to the tent to check out. They were the last responders being pulled out of the valley before the storm hit. One spotter remained in the front seat with the pilot, the engine idling, waiting for their final instructions.

The fire chief in the tent clicked on the radio, once the men checked their names off the personnel list and the list was double-checked for accuracy.

"Okay Matt," he radioed to the pilot. "That's everyone, it's been confirmed. You're clear to do a few more runs before sunset, that'll give you about an hour and half before we have to shut it down. How's the fuel?"

"Roger chief, I'm good for another four hours, so we've got plenty of fuel in the tank. What are your instructions?"

"Maybe check the north fork again to see if anyone washed down from the first leg of the storm, then swing along the lower valley ridges one more time before heading back to the airport."

The whine of the jet engine increased to ear splitting intensity, the pop of the propeller pounding the air above the light weight rescue helicopter. It rose two hundred feet straight up into the air, before angling its nose forward and heading back across the river, taking a short cut to the north fork.

A group of thirty bystanders of all shapes and sizes gathered along the river bank next to the tent that a day earlier was a makeshift dressing room for the actors, and banquet hall for the crew, a happy fun place, and was now a grim command center for a rescue operation that now appeared to be turning into a recovery operation.

Everyone gathered around the chief as he made his announcement.

Two film crews from Honolulu jockeyed for position with Paul and Max, both of them wearing Clippers jerseys since the Lakers lost and part of the bet was the loser wearing the winner's shirt for a month.

They'd already gone over procedure long before the chief was ready to give his announcement. Ditch the tripod and go full rogue mobile, edge the other guys out before they knew what hit them. You had to anticipate positioning well in advance, and they were pros, beating the other teams to the perfect spot. Max had the camera, Paul controlled the audio pack. Their bitter sports rivalry on hold while the news story was unfolding in front of them, they were team-mates out to crush the other players. They were battle tested outfoxing squads from New York and Hollywood on the red carpets, and paparazzi guerilla strikes around the top stars. It was all-out dog eat dog mentality. The crews from Honolulu didn't stand a chance. They pulled their on-camera talent with them, like a rugby team in a scrum. Courtney Squires stood nearby. Ready for action. She was a pretty girl, perfect hair and teeth, and also gritty, solid and able to take an elbow and still press forward, always press forward. They were right up front and center as the chief cleared his throat and began to speak.

"Unfortunately we have found no sign of Miss Ashley Pepper. This is hour number twenty six of our search and rescue operation. We've had over one hundred county, state, federal and local volunteers assist with the search. Due to the approach of Hurricane Del we're issuing orders to suspend all operations until the storm passes. The most recent data shows that the center of Del is seventy five miles to the north east of the island and heading directly for us at ten miles an hour. This brings the center of the storm over the island at around midnight tonight. Sustained winds at the center are estimated to be one hundred and ten knots. We are advising everyone to immediately vacate this area and seek shelter. Our remaining team will break down and secure our command tent and resume operations tomorrow morning. Any questions."

Courtney had her question out of her mouth before the chief could finish saying the word question. She looked petite, but was loud and up front. No one else had a chance.

"Chief why are you suspending operations with over two hours of daylight remaining and the storm still almost eight hours away?"

He looked at the offending inquisitor with calm dignity. These kinds of questions were to be expected. More were soon to follow. Especially if there was a disaster, if Ashley and Tom couldn't be found or were found dead, and it was later determined that they could have been found, or if other people died because he didn't order the suspension and they were hurt in the storm, more second guessing would happen. There was no easy way around it. Someone had to make a decision, and it came down to him.

"We still have one helicopter doing a visual grid search, but it was prudent to remove all other personnel from the ground at this time. It's going to be dark soon and we don't want to put any more people at risk."

Courtney was a pro and started shouting out the next question before he could finish. Her voice rang out so loud, in a semi screech, that everyone looked at her in stunned surprise while she yelled it.

"Who gave the order to suspend the search!"

All eyes swiveled to the man in the center of the crowd, everyone turned their attention to the fire chief who frowned.

"I gave the order. At some point in time the

decision has to be made in the interest of public safety. The fire department of this island is in charge of all search and rescue operations, and after careful consultation with the police, Civil Defense, and National Guard, I as acting chief am ordering the suspension of all search and rescue operations until further notice."

I sure as hell hope I'm right, he thought.

Louise had elbowed her way to the front of the crowd with her film crew and finally got in a question.

"Chief, will there be a criminal investigation into Ashley's disappearance?"

He looked over at Grant who was at the edge of the crowd, his bald head unmistakable. He could see the palpable fear on his face.

"You'll have to ask the police department that question. Tomorrow morning at dawn we expect the storm to be out of our area, and we can resume operations. The problem may be, if there's widespread destruction, many people will need assistance. As of now, our main concern is public safety as this storm moves closer. And now ladies and gentlemen we are requesting that everyone vacate this area immediately and seek shelter."

Courtney and Louise, shoulder to shoulder now, jostled to get in a last question but accidently got their elbows locked and were preempted by a tiny shrieking voice down by the river.

A group of children had gathered by the water's edge, unmotivated by the press briefing and were instead concentrating on throwing rocks into the water to see who could throw the farthest. One of them finished throwing his rock with such force that his body turned so violently to the left that he was facing straight up the river and saw the nose of the little yellow kayak heading their way.

"There they are!" he shouted.

Everyone in the crowd turned at the sound of his voice. It turned so silent you could hear a pin drop.

Way up the river, so far away that unless you had young eyes it was just a pin point of yellow was some sort of craft heading down stream.

Louise and Courtney both stopped jostling and also turned to the commotion at the river's edge.

"You gotta be kidding me," whispered Courtney.

Louise was first off the blocks, unlocking her elbow, then grabbing her film crew and pulling them behind her. Courtney held back with Paul and Max as they assessed the situation.

"Alright," she said. "This isn't our first rodeo. They're still a ways away, if in fact that's her. Let's get some wide shots with the crowd in the foreground and the kayak in the background. Then let's think about the second half of the equation which is the most important one."

"Yeah," said Paul. "I think we have about ten or fifteen minutes. Where do we want to be when they get on shore. It's going to be a free for all."

"We definitely *don't* want to be right in the

center of the action," said Max. "Give ourselves some room, we need to see the big picture."

"Okay, think," said Paul. "You've been lost in the valley for the past couple of days, You're coming down the river to safety, you're tired, hungry, maybe half dead. You get to the nearest possible landing site and get on shore as quick as possible." He pointed. "Right there, you see it? That sandy area just to the right of the kid who spotted them. That's the landing zone. That's where we want to be, but just to the outside of the mob that's going to be surrounding them."

"Yeah," said Max. "See that flat rock about twenty feet away from the water? Let's go commander it right now."

Paul handed the audio pack to Max and started jogging towards the rock, he could see the other film crews making plans. One of them turned to see Paul jogging, and as soon as he and Paul's eyes met, Paul broke into a run. The other camera man looked to see where Paul was running, saw the flat rock that was about three feet high and wide enough for two people to stand, smiled and started sprinting for it. He was closer.

Paul however, had another gear. He was a sprinter in high school, specialized in the fifty yard dash, and closed the distance to the rock before the other guy could get there. He was going so fast, over slick muddy ground that he almost miscalculated, and when he tried to slow down so he could step up onto the rock instead of flying by it, his feet began to slide, and he skated the last couple of yards, and flopped chest first on the rock, spread eagled like a giant crab, claiming it. He looked up at the other guy who also slid on the mud and ended up on his tail end, next to the rock, but too late.

"You bastard," the other guy said.

Paul stood triumphant grinning ear to ear as Max joined him on the rock, slugging all the gear. Now they had a perfect shot of the crowd with the kayak in the background, and if he was correct in his calculations, a perfect angle for when they came on-shore.

26.

The little yellow kayak languidly rounded the final bend in the river before the last long straightway to the dock. They could see it in the distance, five hundred yards away.

A slight breeze was at their back, a gentle north wind, remnant of the fast moving storm passage that nearly killed them a few hours ago. A helping wind, along with the river flowing towards the shoreline, Tom estimated they would be on it within a few minutes.

Ashley lounged in the front seat, staring at the clouds, dragging a hand in the water.

"Hey, are you sleeping?" asked Tom.

Her voice was light and peaceful.

"Well, I feel like I'm dreaming, so maybe I am."

"Check it out," he said. "Look at all those people."

She sat up reluctantly, stirred from her woken dream. She hadn't missed throngs pulling at her from every direction. Deadlines and commitments. The solitude of the river was nearly over.

There was a large crowd, all shapes and sizes. They could see TV crews and newspaper reporters with big cameras and microphones swarming around a tent full of black suited SWAT team members, police and firefighters.

No one was watching the river. No one except for a couple of kids. Too short to see what all the commotion was all about, shut out and pushed to the outer edge by the crowd of big people, their attention was focused on the water.

They were all taking turns throwing rocks. A bird swooped down to check the splash in the water, then flew away up the river. The little boy who threw the rock follow its flight path with his eyes, right towards the kayak heading their way.

The chief was talking into a microphone hooked to a speaker so everyone can hear him. The sound carried up the river to the kayak.

A muffled question was shouted from the crowd.

In the silence while the chief tried to formulate an answer, the little boy shouted at the top of his lungs.

"Look! There they are!"

First one person turned to see who was shouting, then as though the entire crowd at once realized what had been shouted, they all turned their attention to top of the river, then pandemonium ensued.

The little boy was nearly trampled as news crews and photographers scrambled to get the best angle of the kayak that was a hundred yards away, slowly making its way towards them.

The red rescue helicopter came zooming across the river, the pilot hanging his head halfway out the door less chopper hovered well to the right of the kayak. He gave Tom the thumbs up, then circled around to land behind the tents.

Mayhem, bedlam, chaos enveloped as over a hundred people crowded the edge of the river to help the two kayakers out of their craft, swarming around them.

Cameras, microphones, boom mics on each side as they made their way through the crowd.

A police siren went off.

Three people fell into the water from the commotion and the push of the crowd.

Tom and Penny struggled to make their way through the mob. It occurred to Penny that it was easier going through the buffalo grass. They were one person falling, one surge of the crowd from being trampled.

The questions rained down on them, reporters frantic to get the scoop, fans trying to get as close as possible.

"Ashley, how'd you get lost?!"

"How did you survive?!"

"Are you injured?!"

"I love you!"

A reporter thrust a microphone in Tom's face.

"How did you find her sir?!"

Ashley was well trained in this type of scene and grabbed Tom's hand, pulling him with her to safety.

They finally got a few feet from the edge of

the river. The producer pummeled his way through the throng, stepped in front of them, thrust his hands in the air, and shouted at the top of his lungs.

"Please everyone, give them some room, one question at a time!"

In the split second of time that ensued, a loud voice boomed from the side.

"Hey Ashley, how was your hike?"

All eyes looked towards Grant, then back at Ashley.

Time stood still.

Face blank, the exhaustion from the past two days fading quickly, body language exuding pure anger, slowly turned her bloodshot eyes towards the voice. She spotted Grant, smiling at her, then gripped Tom's hand tightly and began to make her way towards the offending voice. It was shocking to see the fury in her eyes.

There was utter silence as the crowd parted to make way for her until she was standing right in front of the bald one.

"I'll tell you how my hike was."

She grabbed the paddle from Tom, then with one swift karate chop motion broke the blade over Grant's head.

And that's how the legend started again.

He fell to his knees and she threw the paddle down next to him while the crowd cheered. Most of them didn't even know what they were cheering for, they just knew that they'd witnessed a big-time news event first hand.

Everyone with a cell phone camera thought

they must have gotten the photo of the century, the tabloids were going to have a field day with this shot.

Tom, standing to the side looked on with amazement, shaking his head and sighing.

"Just like the old days," he said.

Max standing on the rock, head and shoulders above the crowd had been filming the whole time.

"Did you get the shot?" Paul shouted in his ear over the roar of the crowd. Max had a grin spread ear to ear as he continued to film, one eye set firm into the eyepiece.

"Oh yeah. Pulitzer prize, here we come."

Paul looked over at the other film crews and smiled, they were all pinned into the crowd by the edge of the river, pinched in the mob and unable to move close enough to get the shot as it happened.

Courtney was moving into position and Paul hopped down off the rock with the audio backpack, weaved his way through the crowd and handed her the microphone.

Ashley recognized her, realized that she'd have to give at least one short interview to get everyone off her back so she could get out of there. The ferocity of smashing the paddle over her tormentor's head had a strange calming effect on her. Vengeance had been taken and it was sweet.

Just as Courtney was about to ask a question, the chief of police held up his hand palm first in front of Ashley to hold still while another officer brought Grant to her side.

Courtney circled her finger in the air for Max to keep filming, and she held the mic close to the group to record the voices.

"Both of you," said the chief. "Have the right to press charges against the other. Miss Pepper, you were assaulted yesterday at the waterfall by this gentleman, do you wish to press charges?"

She studied Grant's face for a moment. Maybe she was a little bit stressed when he tried to kiss her and flew off the handle. Besides, if none of that happened, she wouldn't have gotten lost, and found the person whose hand she was still gripping tightly.

"No," she said finally. "I do not want to press charges."

"What about you Grant? You want to press charges against Miss Pepper for assault?"

Grant stood motionless for a moment studying Ashley. He now had complete control over her fate. Everyone saw her whack him with the paddle. Why, he could even claim some sort of physical condition that would carry him to the end of his days in luxury. Develop a slight tic, drool unexpectedly, shout out gibberish for no reason, jump up and down like he was walking on hot coals. But he could sense the crowd mummering around him, there was an electric buzz in the air, and he was no dummy. Press charges against Pepper for something she was pretty much entitled to do would be the end of him. There wouldn't be any charges filed by either one of them. Right before he was going to give his answer he thought briefly about saying that he wouldn't press charges if he could get one real kiss from her, but he rubbed the top of his head and could feel the bump staring to rise. She was pretty much as tough in person as she was on film. After all it was just a little paddle, the next time might be an anvil.

"Nope, no charges from me."

The crowd who were silent, waiting for the answer, erupted in cheers.

Grant held out his fist towards Ashley, and she gently bumped knuckles against his. What the heck she figured, she could always disinfect her hand, and it wasn't as bad as having spiders climb across her neck. She shivered at the thought. Tom was getting wise to the protocol in the current situation, stuck in a crowd, and decided to take charge, he re-gripped Ashley's hand and semi-dragged her with him through the edge and into free space.

He was impressed with the speed at which she walloped Grant, and whispered into her ear.

"Remind me never to piss you off."

She elbowed him in the ribs and re-clutched his hand. The producer was at the other side of Ashley acting as an additional wedge.

"Who's he?"

"This is Tom. Tom, this is Mitchell Collins, the director."

They both shook hand across her waist as they continued to walk quickly. They were headed to the white limo next to the tent.

"We've got your bags in the car," said Mitchell. "All the airlines are grounded with the hurricane on the way."

They all stopped and the crowd began to filter back around them, hemming them in.

"There's a hurricane?" said Ashley.

"Yes, a category two, it formed quickly last night, and it's about eight hours away, supposed to be a direct hit. We thought we were going to lose you. They were wrapping up the command post and getting everyone to shelter when you miraculously showed up. I must admit you seem to have a flair for the dramatic."

"What about that giant rain and lightning storm earlier today?" asked Tom.

"That was just a little band that twirled off the main storm," said Mitchell. "A little snack before the main course. Now as I was saying Ashley, the airlines are grounded so you're going to have to stay here tonight. We have a suite booked at the best hotel on the island, there's a hurricane shelter in the hotel, solid concrete and steel. Your bags are in the limo."

She shook her head. "I'm staying with Tom."

Both Tom and Mitchell looked at her in surprise, but it was Tom who spoke first.

"You are?"

She was all business.

"Of course I am, now where's your truck? Let's get the kayak and get the heck out of here."

Twenty people had pens and papers in their hands, practically begging for an autograph, but it was a little girl around seven years old, missing a front tooth, and her big brother who looked around eight, hovering around her knees that stopped her.

"Okay," she let go of Tom's hand. "You go get the truck, and I'll sign autographs for a while okay?"

"Yes boss," Tom grinned, still in shock from the news just a moment ago that she wanted to stay with him. For the past two days he figured he'd get her safely out of the valley and that would be the end of it.

She bent down at the little girls level to have a talk and sign her paper while Tom headed up to the parking lot to get the truck.

A team of county workers were taking down the command center tent, working as fast as possible.

Tom's buddy from fire rescue, Kane walked over and shook his hand.

"Well congratulations, you're the hero."

"Not me, I just happened to stumble across her trail and she followed me out. I was just minding my own business."

"Where'd you find her."

"Third valley over from Secret Waterfall."

"Deep. No wonder we couldn't find you. We didn't think she got that far over. I haven't been up there in a long time."

"Me neither."

"How'd you get out? Back over the ridge?"

"Down the stream."

"Over the two waterfalls?"

"Yep."

Kane whistled.

"I think the last time we went up there was

around the first year of high school. Scared the hell out of me going down those cliffs."

"It hasn't gotten any easier."

"I have a question for you. Just something I was wondering."

"What's that?"

"How come you didn't just light a big smoky fire? We could have found you in a few minutes."

Tom looked at Kane with a blank face, eyelids slightly drooping, and shrugged his shoulders.

"You know I never thought of it. Maybe I'm not as smart as I look."

Kane kept looking at Tom, studying his face. And then he knew.

"Why you sly dog. You kept her on purpose out there with you."

"I'm shocked that you would think such a thing."

Kane held up his hands, palms forward in defense.

"Hey, it doesn't matter to me one way or the other. You didn't have any matches, the wood was wet, there's no flint type stones in Hawaii, there's all kinds of reasons why you couldn't light a fire. Me and the boys, we don't mind hiking around out in the jungle looking for you, gives us a reason to get outside and we need the exercise right? I'm just thinking how some of the powers that be might take it."

Tom's eyes drifted back to Ashley with her back towards him, talking to the crowd gathered around her, signing autographs. A big movie star again.

"You know I don't like building fires up there. Never did. A couple of embers might drift away, and next thing you know I accidently burn the whole place down. Now that would really piss off the powers that be. I've got my little sterno tins and that's it. A little tiny pinpoint flame that can't get out of control. But, in hindsight, if ever there was a time to make a big smoky fire, yesterday would have been the day. Right before the deluge."

"I understand Tom. I was just pulling your leg. Remember that time when we were kids and decided to make a little bonfire up there? Right around sunset in the first valley. We must have been about ten or eleven, real mountain men. Smiley kicked one of the embers by accident, it rolled into a pile of leaves and lit that thing up like it exploded. You grabbed all our sleeping bags and threw them on top and stomped it out before it could get out of control. We spent a miserable night but you prevented a disaster. Right then and there, that's when I decided to be a fireman."

Tom popped him on the shoulder.

"Good choice."

He continued onto the parking lot and located the old truck, found the keys on the back axle, checked the tires, grabbed a gallon container from the bed, popped the hood, added water to the radiator, then hopped inside and fired up the engine. It rumbled to life, grey smoke at first out the tailpipe, the engine grumbling for a while, then smoothing out to an even hum.

The crowd was thinning as he drove down to the water's edge, and loaded up the kayak on the metal racks, tying it down with bungee cords. He looked around for the broken paddle but it was long gone. Someone probably took it home for a souvenir. It'd be hanging over their mantle before sundown.

27.

They rambled down the dirt road to the end of the cul-de-sac, pulling up in front of the little tin roofed shack. The sun was getting low on the horizon, the thick wall of clouds from the storm loomed in the distance.

Two hungry cats heard the familiar old truck coming from miles away, and stuck their noses out from the thick red and purple flowered bougainvillea ringing the old porch.

"This is your house?" said Ashley.

After all they'd been through Tom couldn't figure out from the inflection of her voice whether she was severely disappointed, or slightly disillusioned. It didn't really matter. It was a simple question, and she sounded surprised, who wouldn't, but on what side of the reaction was her heart? Surprised as in holy cow what have I gotten into, this guy lives like a damn hillbilly, or surprised as in oh well it just needs a little fixing up. Sure they'd been through an ordeal up in the valley, but that was in the past. In the real world she was a super-rich movie star that was used to being pampered. Expected it.

He looked at her and sighed, shrugging his

shoulders.

"Yep, that's my house. A little rough around the edges, kind of like me I guess. It could use a little paint and maybe a new roof. But it's been through two hurricanes, without a scratch, without so much as losing a single board, so the builders back in their day must have been doing something right. C'mon, let's check it out."

He looked at her suitcase in the back of the truck, started to reach for it, then decided to leave it there if she didn't want to stay.

They climbed the stairs up onto the porch, the cats were wary at first, but their hunger at not being fed for a night and a day won out.

They came meowing out of their hiding spot arching their backs, rubbing against Tom's legs, begging for food. Ashley bent down and scratched the thin haired grey tiger striped cat under the chin, while the giant fluffy white one waited for its turn.

"That's Tiger, I call the white one Big Harry."

"I can see why."

She stood up, looking at all the hard details around her, the house, the cul-de-sac, the giant old trees. She had a far off look in her eyes, the same one that he noticed up in the valley as she surveyed the scene next to the river while they ate their lunch, taking in not only the actual physical view, but trying to feel the vibrations from the surroundings.

"We can stay here," he said. "Or I can take you to the hotel where you'll be safer. Your call. I should probably stay with these little fur balls to make sure they don't get in trouble. I owe them that. It's too late to get them to a shelter, and the hotel wouldn't allow it."

Ever the gentleman, extending an exit door, an easy way out, no worries, no regrets, no drama if she had second thoughts about staying with him. It was the right thing to do. The only thing to do. He'd take her to a hotel and that would be that. End of story. What happened in the valley would fade into a cute little memory. Something she could tell her friends throughout the years, before it finally faded away to nothing.

She shook her head and took him by the hand. Energy beaming from her face, pure ecstatic contentment.

"This is perfect. I actually love, love, *love* it. This house has so much character, it's like a scene from an old movie."

She tapped him on the chin with her forefinger, very lightly.

"You're like a scene from an old movie. They don't make 'em like you anymore Thomas O'Malley. You're not getting rid of me *that* easy. Now let's go get my suitcase that you conveniently left in the truck, and go inside and get ready for the hurricane."